Welcome to the Hush Hotel!
Check out the couple in room 1864...

"Touch me," Kit whispered, straddling his lap.

Peter didn't have to be asked twice. He reached for her breasts, tracing the shape of them through the silk, loving the textures, the nipples pebbling against his fingertips.

He pictured her lushly painted mouth as she murmured, "What will happen next?"

Paper crackled. " 'Will she let me love her?' " Her voice was low and sexy as she read. " 'I don't know. It's her choice. Her decision.'" He heard his own words written for the fantasy contest, though she'd added a few of her own.

He hadn't realized how intense his need would be, with the woman he was in love with—had loved forever—splayed across his lap.

Kit kissed him suddenly, and the shock of her lips, glossy and wet, felt like his first kiss ever.

"Let me love you," he gasped. "Now."

"Yes..."

There was no way the chair could hold them, what with the two of them tearing at each other's clothes. They tumbled off and onto the floor—the plush, deeply carpeted, made-for-rolling-around-having-wild-sex floor.

Blaze™

Dear Reader,

Harlequin Blaze books always involve an element of fantasy. Get half a dozen Blaze authors together and the fantasies really start to fly. Talented Jo Leigh was the inspiration behind the DO NOT DISTURB series, which takes place in Manhattan's newest boutique hotel, Hush.

She invited a few of us to join her and the fun began. Authors Isabel Sharpe, Alison Kent, Jill Shalvis, Debbi Rawlins and myself had a wonderful time designing and populating the hotel.

I decided to make my heroine an overambitious but extremely talented public relations director for Hush. The hero is her own personal PR disaster and an unwelcome surprise in her life. But you can't put two wildly attracted people together in a hotel like Hush and not see sparks. Or fireworks. *Private Relations* was a great project to work on with a wonderful group of writers.

For more on the series, including contests and behind-the-scenes info, please visit www.Hush.com. I hope you'll also check out the free online DO NOT DISTURB stories at eHarlequin.com. And stop by to visit me at www.nancywarren.net.

Check in to Hush and enjoy the fun.

Nancy Warren

NANCY WARREN
Private Relations

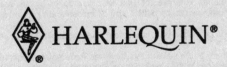

HARLEQUIN®

TORONTO • NEW YORK • LONDON
AMSTERDAM • PARIS • SYDNEY • HAMBURG
STOCKHOLM • ATHENS • TOKYO • MILAN • MADRID
PRAGUE • WARSAW • BUDAPEST • AUCKLAND

Private Relations is dedicated to three of my personal favorite relations: my nieces. To Madeleine, Dominique and the newest addition to our family, Charlotte. With love from your Auntie Nancy.

ISBN 0-373-79213-1

PRIVATE RELATIONS

Copyright © 2005 by Nancy Warren.

www.eHarlequin.com

Printed in U.S.A.

1

KIT PRESTCOTT strode through the lobby of Hush Hotel with the two essentials of her trade—her cell, currently glued to her ear, and her determined smile, currently glued to her face.

As public relations director of Manhattan's hot new boutique hotel, Kit spent a lot of time on the phone, and she'd perfected that smile. No matter what might be going on behind the scenes, she'd developed that smile as shield, weapon and smoke screen.

A gossip columnist had once called her, "Kit Prestcott, the human equivalent of those Smiley Face emoticons that litter e-mail messages like so many fleas." Instead of being insulted, Kit had laughed and taken to collecting Smiley Face memorabilia.

"The flowers in the lobby aren't as fresh as I'd like," she told one of Manhattan's top florists, who was going to be lucky to sell daisies at a farmer's market if she let word slip that she wasn't happy with his product, and he knew it.

Tough. There was no excuse in Kit's mind for not doing the best job every time. Ambition, creativity, organizational skills: why go into business if you didn't have oodles of all three?

The art deco lobby was so glorious that the slight wilt

to the birds-of-paradise in today's supposedly fresh arrangement irked her unbearably. While chastising the florist, she mentally flicked through ideas for the big promotion she was planning for RAJ Jewelry's unveiling of its fall line. It was a prestigious and glam show that Kit had worked her butt off to get, and she was determined the event would be so spectacular that the company would automatically book Hush for all its exclusive launch parties.

As though her brain had a PowerPoint presentation loaded in, an elephant appeared in a full-colored slide—what better way to make a grand entrance for the finest Indian sapphires and rubies than to have an Indian elephant lumber in carrying a maharaja and a treasure chest. Ooh, that could be good. Silk tents, maybe a bazaar theme...

But where was she going to get an elephant in Manhattan? And could elephants be housebroken, or would she have to deal with an elephant-sized diaper?

Dream big was her motto, and okay, so maybe sometimes her dreams were a little over the top. That Amazon scene she'd created in her last job to promote a new South American Fair Trade Certified coffee had been perfect. Every snaking green vine and tree leaf had been in place; she'd borrowed several tame parrots from a pet shop to sit in those trees. She'd even managed a lagoon complete with live crocodiles. There'd been salsa music and delicious South American cuisine, and the enticing aroma of coffee beans had perfumed the air.

How was she to have known that the crocodiles would try to snack on the parrots, who didn't seem to know how to fly, and that in the melee, the barrier would give out, sending the crocs sliding into the packed ballroom?

As the dreadful memory assailed her, the elephant in her mental PowerPoint presentation disappeared as though her internal hard drive had crashed.

Cancel the elephant.

"I'm saying the flowers weren't as fresh as I expected," she said, continuing her cellular argument with that arrogant ass of a florist.

"You ask for birds-of-paradise out of season, what do you expect?"

"I expect that they will be fresh and perfect. That's what we're paying for." She didn't snarl or shout; that smile stayed plastered on her face, even though the florist couldn't see her. Pleasant. Always pleasant and friendly, but never willing to settle for less than the best. That was how to get what you wanted.

She passed the concierge desk and waved to the pink-haired concierge who was helping a young couple book tickets to a Broadway play. A successful-looking businessman was reading *The Wall Street Journal* in one of the seafoam-green chairs while his much younger female companion flipped through a book of erotica from the Hush library. *Doomed relationship ahead.*

A lone bartender polished glasses in Erotique, preparing for the prelunch crowd.

The leaded-glass front door swung open to admit a woman in a faux fur coat and tippy-tappy stiletto heels. One of the black-uniformed porters followed behind with her matched set of Louis Vuitton luggage, so Kit assumed the faux fur was a moral choice rather than a financial one. Idly, she wondered who the woman was meeting and if she was wearing anything under that coat.

By this time, Kit had extracted a grudging "I'll see what I can do" from the florist.

"Today would be great," she said with her usual cheerfulness and ended the call as she reached the elevator that she rode down to the basement where the hotel's owner, Piper Devon, had her office. From her briefcase, Kit extracted the batch of entries she'd received for the Hush Fantasy Weekend Contest promotion. She frowned slightly as the elevator doors opened. The fantasy weekend had been her idea, her baby—odd that Piper would insist on being involved. Were those damned crocodiles still stalking her career?

Determined that nothing would spoil her success in this job, or Hush's success, since she knew how important the venture was to Piper, she decided to be grateful that the hotel owner was going to help her choose the very first Fantasy Weekend winner.

She said "Hi" to Angela Portero, Piper's secretary, who waved her into Piper's office.

She breezed in and found her old friend and new boss standing in front of the architect's renderings of the lobby. Piper was movie-star gorgeous and to those who didn't know her, could come across as an empty-headed playgirl—but Kit had known her a long time and never made that mistake. Piper stared at those drawings the way a new mother would stare at a newborn.

"Still can't believe you pulled it off?" Kit asked softly.

Piper turned and laughed. "I swear, sometimes I wake up in the middle of the night and think I just had the craziest dream that I opened an erotic boutique hotel."

"Yeah, well, I've got some people who dream of staying here."

"Ooh," Piper squealed, her eyes lighting. "Have you got the entries?"

Piper looked so excited that Kit immediately discounted her earlier suspicion that her boss was going to be riding her tail constantly. The woman was obviously thrilled about the promo and wanted to play a part, however small.

"Yep. I weeded out the total grossoes whose fantasies would make you gag. Here are the rest of the contenders for the fantasy weekend promotion. Some male, some female."

"Cool," Piper said, moving to the cream leather sectional and sitting down beside Eartha Kitty. The hotel cat curled up in the corner, a hint of her sparkly pink collar showing. When the couch shifted as the women sat, she opened one sleepy green eye, then closed it again.

Kit placed the stack of entries on the table.

Of course, she'd already read all of them, and of course she'd already made her selection. If she couldn't call on all her persuasive skills to influence Piper to come to the same decision, then she needed to get out of PR.

At Piper's insistence, the entries were anonymous. It seemed ridiculous to Kit—but Piper was a perfectionist, and she was the boss—so the entries had all gone to Piper's assistant, been numbered and then sent to Kit. Naturally, Angela had also indicated whether the entrant was male or female, since part of the prize was a host or hostess to make the all-expenses-paid weekend memorable.

The selection of the hosts had been tricky. She wanted absolutely nothing skanky and had deliberately elected to use the term host/ess over escort. The chosen ones were all young, attractive, interesting people who loved Manhattan and knew it inside and out. The hosts—a lot of whom were people she knew—received a fantastic weekend, including their own room in the hotel, and a nice fat check at the end of the weekend.

They were all single and not dating anyone exclusively. While sex was in no way part of the package, well, Hush was a sensual paradise and people sometimes became attracted to one another. Kit didn't want any broken hearts as a result of one of her promotions.

She'd already suffered one of those herself, and no one knew better how painful it could be. In her case, the event she'd so meticulously organized that had ended in a broken heart had been her own wedding. With a quick shudder, she turned her attention back to the stack of pages Piper was flipping through, gazing from one to the next as though they were Godiva chocolates and she couldn't decide which to sink her teeth into first.

"I don't know where to start," Piper said, pushing the pages back to her. "Why don't you read the entries aloud?"

"Some of them are a little…intimate," she said, thinking of her choice for their first winner, and how his words had curled up her spine when she'd read them. Entry number twenty-four sounded like a man she wouldn't mind getting to know. In fact, she'd already decided that when he arrived to claim his prize, she'd hang around the hotel long enough to introduce herself.

"Well, how about we both take turns reading them aloud? That way we can discuss them."

"All right." She fanned the pages out on the table, then grinned suddenly at her old friend. "You're the experienced party girl. You first." Piper was now a respectable hotelier in love with a decent man and utterly happy with her newfound stability, but her wild-child past would always be part of her. And of Hush.

"Fine." Piper trailed her French-manicured fingernails in the air above the entries and chose one.

"This one's from a woman. All right. What's her fantasy?" Piper glanced up. "What did they have to do again?"

"In two hundred words, describe one fantasy you'd like to fulfill while staying at Manhattan's sensual boutique hotel, Hush," she recited from the entry form they'd placed in national papers and magazines and selected radio stations.

"My fantasy," Piper read, "is to spend the entire weekend naked." She glanced up. "I thought you were weeding out the wackos? We are pretty broad-minded at Hush, but I can't have people treating it like a nudist colony."

"Read on."

With a raised eyebrow, she did. "I'd sleep naked between the finest sheets. I'd awaken naked and order room service. Naturally, I'd put on a robe to let the room service waiter in, but underneath my robe, I'd be naked. He'd know it and I'd know it." Piper put down the page on the right-hand side of the table.

"Great. This chick wants to prance around in her birthday suit and do the room service waiters—I'm starting a No pile and she's in it." Then she turned to Kit and settled back. "Tag, you're it."

Kit could see number twenty-four in the middle of the fan. Not yet, she told herself. She wanted Piper to pull that one so Kit chose another.

"This is from a guy," she said, then read, "My fantasy is to find that special woman and make slow, passionate love to her on a bearskin rug in front of a crackling fire." She glanced up. "Shall I go on?"

"Trapper John there not only belongs in the Appalachians, but he's got no imagination. Bearskin rug?" Piper shook her head. "Send him back to the Eighties. I hope these get better."

They did. Some craved bondage, some exhibitionism. One energetic guy wanted to have sex in every room of the hotel, but he had such a humorous and lusty take on sex that they put him with the Yeses, anyway.

A comedienne with a Cinderella fantasy had them both laughing aloud at her witty, and yet heartfelt entry. She went in the Yes pile, right at the top. She was definitely going to be one of the four winners, to win one of a month of fantasy weekends, but Kit really hoped that number twenty-four would get the most special of the prizes—the first weekend.

As the pile dwindled, there were half a dozen entries in the Yes file, and many more in the No pile. Kit's fingers itched to reach for her favorite entry, but she held back, wanting Piper to be the one to read it. Finally, they were down to two and it was Piper's turn. Her hand hovered and then chose entry forty-seven, from a woman whose fantasy was simply to be pampered, away from work and all distractions. She wanted to hole up in a luxury suite, eat food she didn't have to cook and be left alone to relax.

"Now there's a fantasy I can relate to," Piper admitted when she'd finished reading.

"Me, too," Kit agreed.

"When did we turn into such workaholics?" Piper asked. Then grinned. "Okay, for me it was when I decided to stick it to Daddy and open my own hotel." She laughed. "Best decision I ever made."

"It sure was." Then Kit sighed, thinking about her own workaholic tendencies. "I've always been driven."

"Worse since your wedding day," Piper said gently.

"I'll read the last one," Kit said, snatching entry twenty-four up so fast she gave herself a paper cut.

"You never talk about him," Piper said.

They'd been friends too long for her to pretend she didn't know whom Piper was referring to. The three of them had gone to school together—Piper, the girl born with the silver spoon in her mouth and carrying a mountain of painful baggage; Kit, the go-getter with the scholarship and relentless energy; and Peter, the charming, athletic business major she'd loved and planned to marry.

"I never dwell on past mistakes. I've moved on. If I talked about him it would give him importance in my life, and he has none."

She turned her attention back to the entry in her hands and began to read.

Hush. I hear that word and I think of night falling, sharing whispered secrets, making slow, intimate love while the rest of the world sleeps, then the quiet breathing of a well-loved woman lying beside me in the night. What secrets would I whisper to her? What fantasy would I share? It is this: the woman I dream about is so confident of her sexuality, so sure of her own power, that she's not afraid to give up control completely to a man she trusts, or to take control if that is her desire.

I picture this woman walking into my hotel room in an elegant black dress and high heels that make her legs long and sleek. Her hair is up. She looks like she's going to some classy dinner. She doesn't say a word, but points to a chair. I sit. And

watch. There are mirrors in the room. She doesn't
look at herself, but at me. I can see her reflected,
though, from all sides. Slowly, she unzips her
dress, peels it off and she's got more black, but it's
stripper stuff. A thong, a see-through bra, a garter
belt and stockings. She teases me slowly as she
undresses, so I only see a little at a time, and all
those reflections drive me mad. If I try to rise and
join her, she stops and shakes her head. No. Not
yet. I can barely stay on my chair. I wish she'd tied
me there so I wouldn't have to control myself, but
she hasn't. She stops me with a glance. I can see
her, smell her, and it's killing me not to touch her,
taste her, take her.

She's close to naked, but still wearing that sexy
underwear when she comes closer and straddles
my lap. Yes, I think. Finally. She undoes my tie,
slips it out of my collar and then before I know
what she's got in mind, she's putting it over my
eyes and tying it behind my head.

Kit had to stop and take a breath. She felt hot and
cold chills running over her skin and grabbed at the
bottle of water Piper had placed on the table and
gulped.

"No," I say. I want to see her, but she only laughs,
then she takes my hands and lets me touch her.
She lets me take off her bra, and it's killing me because I can't see her. I feel as if I've known this
woman forever, and that I've never met her. I
touch her skin and feel the heat coming off her, I
touch her intimate places and know she wants me.

Will she let me love her? I don't know. I'm in agony, but it's up to her.

When she was finished reading, Kit felt uncomfortable warmth prickling her own intimate places. She glanced up at Piper who said, "That was more than two hundred words."

And suddenly they were giggling like the schoolgirls they'd been when they first met.

"I can't believe it. He sounds so hot," Kit said at last.

"That made me hot," Piper agreed.

"So?"

Piper considered, with her head to one side. "The stand-up comedian woman with the Cinderella scenario is more of a PG-13 fantasy."

"While the man's is more in tune with the Hush concept of erotic indulgence." Kit sighed. "The hostess doesn't have to fulfill his fantasy, of course, but I think he's the kind of client we want in the hotel. He's sensual and not afraid to show it. He obviously likes women, and he has no problem giving up control." She laughed. "I wish more men were like that."

Piper gazed at her for another long moment. "Okay. I hear what you're saying." She nodded briskly. "I think we found our first winner. Let Angela know. She'll set it all up."

Kit nodded and put the entry in a red file folder. Frankly, she wanted to know what happened next in Mr. Twenty-Four's fantasy.

2

PETER GARSON felt an unfamiliar weight in his belly as he punched a number into his cell. It took him a minute to recognize that he was nervous. He was standing in Grand Central Station surrounded by noise and bodies rushing about. He was meeting a client for lunch at the Oyster Bar but first, he had a call to make.

"Well?" he asked when the woman he was calling identified herself.

"If you hurt her again, I swear I will come after you, cut off your balls and feed them to my cat."

"You did it." He leaned against one of the marble pillars sagging in relief.

"I did it," she said. "And you'd better be right about this." She hung up before he could reply.

Feeling better by the second, he strode into the Oyster Bar and found the man he was meeting sipping a gin and tonic with one solitary ice cube in it. "Am I late?" he asked, grasping Giles Pendleton's hand as the older man rose to greet him.

"Not at all. I was early. You look rather pleased with yourself. Are you about to sign another big client?"

"No. I'm trying to woo a woman."

The older man raised his brows. "Not an impossible proposition I'd guess. You appear to be a good catch to me."

"Thanks, Giles. But this woman's going to be a challenge."

"Why? Did you put her out of business?"

"No. I broke her heart."

"How dramatic."

"Believe me, it was. I left her standing at the altar on our wedding day."

Giles slowly lowered his glass and leveled a shrewd gaze at him. "I wouldn't have believed you to be a cad."

He winced at the term. Old fashioned it might be, but he couldn't argue with the way it hit the mark. "I panicked, Giles. I was on the way to the church and somehow I missed the turning. I figured I'd turn around at the next intersection. Three states later, I realized I wasn't going back."

Giles leaned back looking elegant and amused at the same time, as only the British can. "And you believe you've got a hope in hell with this woman?"

"No." He paused to order a martini for himself, then, when the waiter had left, said, "But I've been thinking a lot lately that I need to see her in person. To apologize."

"You haven't started one of those twelve-step programs you Americans are so fond of, have you? Where you must find everyone you've hurt and embarrass both parties with a tearful making of amends?"

Peter laughed in spite of himself. Giles was two decades older than he was, unimaginably rich and discreetly gay. With so little in common, he was amazed that they'd become and stayed such good friends. "No. It just feels like something I need to do."

Giles slipped a one-hundred-dollar bill from a slim

leather wallet and placed it on the table. "A hundred says she refuses to see you."

Peter grinned and pushed the bill back toward his lunch companion. "I can't take your money, Giles. The meeting's already arranged."

"How poor-spirited of the lady," Giles said, shaking his head and replacing his cash.

"Oh, not entirely. You see, she doesn't know she's going to be seeing me again."

"Well," said Giles, raising his glass in a mock toast. "Isn't she in for a delightful surprise."

"WHAT DO YOU MEAN, Cassie hasn't shown up yet?" Kit said into the phone. She didn't shriek, though she was sorely tempted. "I confirmed with her this morning that she'd host our first fantasy weekend. This is an actress's dream. She gets to be photographed, seen at all the best places. She'll be news, not to mention that we're paying her enough for the weekend to fund her next term in film school. What more does she want?"

"There's more bad news." Helen, the front desk manager, had called Kit herself. Everyone knew how important this promotion was.

"The hotel's on fire?" She meant it sarcastically, but the idea held some immediate appeal. In a disaster, no one would notice that her first big event for Hush since the opening was falling flat on its face. Along with her career.

"Your fantasy weekend winner has checked in already."

"Oh, great." Compared to this, a hotel fire would be a cinch from a public relations standpoint. She checked her Happy Face watch and for once it didn't make her happy. "He's not due for another hour."

"Well, we couldn't turn him away. Besides, he's a cutie. If you need a volunteer to take Cassie's place…"

"No. Thanks. I've got it covered." If only.

She put one knee on her computer chair, hit a key to disperse the Happy Face screen saver and started hammering at the computer trying to dredge up another perfect hostess on a busy Friday afternoon.

"How's it going?"

Normally, Kit was delighted to see Piper, but not right this second when her world was momentarily black and panic was knocking at the door. "Great," she said, sticking a big fake smile on her face as she turned.

"Excellent. Everything all ready for our fantasy bachelor?"

Some people, Kit could lie to if she had to. It turned out that Piper was not one of them. "He's checked in already."

"Wonderful. Did he and Cassie hit it off?"

In the ensuing silence, Kit heard the hum of her computer and the sound of her own blood pressure rising. Finally she gave it up and let her shoulders slump. "She's AWOL. Cassie's AWOL."

"What?" Piper's eyes widened and she shook her head until her hair swung, as though refusing to believe the news. "Where is she? What happened?"

"I don't know. I confirmed with her this morning, and then she didn't show up. No one can get hold of her." Kit frowned.

"Maybe she had an accident or something."

"Maybe."

"What are we going to do?" Piper rarely sounded like the spoiled rich kid she'd once been, but at the moment she did. Kit turned in surprise, but Piper wasn't looking at her, she was scrabbling inside her handbag.

"I'm working on—"

"I'm going to phone a couple of my friends right now. This is insane. What man wants a solo fantasy weekend? We'll be the laughing stock of the city!"

Kit watched in horror as Piper flipped open her cell. You never knew with Piper's friends. Besides, who would be available at five o'clock on a Friday night? Unless they were social losers, or workaholics like Kit.

"Who are you calling?"

"Mimsy. Since her last breakup, she's been pretty down. This will cheer her up."

"Mimsy's in rehab."

"Didn't I tell you? She checked herself out on Wednesday. I get the feeling she's ready to party."

Mimsy. God, no. The only thing worse than Mimsy right before she went into rehab was Mimsy right after she got out. Anything was better than that.

"Put the phone away," she said to Piper more sharply than she intended. "I already have a replacement."

Piper glanced up but didn't close her phone. "Who?"

Kit took a deep breath. "Me. As the PR director, this is my responsibility." Besides, when she stopped steaming about Cassie, she recalled how much she'd liked the sound of this guy. Working this weekend might not be such a hardship after all.

Piper did not appear thrilled. "But you're not a party girl."

"We're not looking for a party girl. This woman is to be a hostess and escort. An interesting and fun person who knows Manhattan."

"And you're wearing that business suit for the intimate dinner tonight in the restaurant?"

Damn it. The *Times* had promised to send a photographer to catch the fantasy weekend winner enjoying a sumptuous intimate dinner in Amuse Bouche. Publicity like that you couldn't buy. "Of course not. I'll run down to the boutique and grab something."

Piper nodded. "Okay, good plan." She scanned Kit from head to toe. "You're out on the town a lot, know everyone, get mentioned in gossip columns. It's perfect, when you think about it."

"Good. I'll go find a dress, then."

"I'm coming with you."

"Why?"

"Because I have great taste in clothes, and this is going on my expense account."

In one of her bold strokes of genius, Piper had hired top fashion designers to decorate the interiors of the penthouses. Of course, Piper being Piper, she'd made sure the high-end lobby boutique carried clothing from those same designers.

"Your fantasy winner's in the Carnaby Suite, right?" Piper said as she gazed around the boutique moments later. "Stella McCartney designed that one. Here, try this." And with her usual crazy-like-a-fox logic, she outfitted Kit in a Stella McCartney dress.

"There. Now you'll match the decor."

"I can't believe you'd spend that much money to make me a room accessory," Kit said as she slipped into a swirling turquoise cocktail dress with indigo polka dots.

"Turn, turn," Piper said, watching critically as she obeyed. "Excellent. Shoes and bag, and we'll be out of here."

The fussing didn't end there. Piper took Kit up to her own suite and insisted on doing her makeup.

"Stop it, I don't wear as much makeup as you do,"

Kit said, batting away a brush full of something dark that appeared headed for her eyelids.

"Think about seeing your picture in the *Times*. Do you want to look washed out and tired? Which is it going to be? Gwyneth Paltrow the day after she gave birth or Gwyneth at a movie premiere?"

"Okay, okay." She let Piper have her way, reminding herself that the dramatic makeup would definitely show up better in any media coverage. "The sacrifices I make for you."

Once Piper had completed the makeup application with a deep pink lipstick, she pulled the hot rollers from Kit's hair and brushed it out. "Gorgeous," she said, and Kit, gazing at her own reflection in Piper's vanity mirror, had to agree she looked…sexy.

Piper slipped the big hotel towel from around Kit's shoulders and handed her the bright pink clutch purse and matching shoes.

After looking her up and down, Piper gave her a quick kiss. "You look great. Good luck!"

"Thanks," Kit said and headed out the door, the cocktail dress floating sexily around her.

She'd feel guilty about wearing a small fortune if she didn't think they'd get that much and more back in advertising value if she could get a mention about the boutique in the paper.

Okay, so for one weekend she was acting a part in her own promotion. Things could be a lot worse. At least now, she didn't have to worry about Cassie screwing up.

Her smile was as carefree as possible given the stress level of its owner as she sped to the eighteenth floor and walked down the lushly carpeted hallway to the Carnaby Suite where she took a moment to take a deep breath and center herself before knocking.

The door opened.

"Hi," said the attractive dark-haired man standing on the other side wearing a crisp white shirt, navy blue slacks and a tie that needed knotting.

For a moment everything went still. She couldn't breathe, her heart didn't seem to beat. She couldn't hear anything. In that instant, she was standing in her wedding gown, reliving the moment when she'd finally accepted she'd been jilted at the altar. She stared at the man she'd planned to marry. She hadn't seen him in the three years since the night before their wedding day. Such a barrage of emotions slammed into her that she couldn't process any of them.

Another woman might have railed, or fainted, or kicked him in a strategic spot. Not Kit, even though she felt like doing all three. Her famous smile wobbled a little, but she hung on to it, just as she hung on to the pink clutch that started to slide out of her grip.

"Peter," she said. "What a surprise."

"Kit. It's good to see you." An awkward moment passed when he didn't move back or speak but simply stared at her. She glanced at the discreet bronze plaque announcing that this was indeed the Carnaby Suite.

So what if Peter turning out to be the winner was a cruel cosmic stroke of fate. There was no way she was going to falter in front of her ex-fiancé. After all, she had faced a ballroom filled with shrieking patrons scrambling to get out of the way of crocodiles reveling in their new-found freedom. One snake she could handle. "So, do I take it you are the lucky winner of the fantasy weekend?"

He seemed to pull himself together with an effort. "Yes. I'm thrilled." He stood back. "Come in."

"Thanks." She was thinking fast as she stepped into the luxurious, sensuously appointed suite with the man she'd once planned to spend her life with. There was no way she could bail on dinner tonight, not with the *Times* photographer coming. But tomorrow, as another famously jilted woman once said, was another day.

"I'm here to take you to dinner," she said briskly, then raised her brows in a challenge. "Is that a problem?"

"There's no one I'd rather have dinner with," he said. *Bite me.* "Fine. Anytime you're ready to go."

"Look. Would you like to have a drink here first? Maybe we should talk before we go out into public together."

She simply looked at him and let her brows ride higher. Soon they'd take off in flight.

He fiddled with the ends of his tie. "In case there are any hard feelings you want to get off your chest. From before."

"By *before,* I assume you mean when you left me standing at the altar on our wedding day?"

He nodded, and she had the satisfaction of seeing a reddening above his collar that meant he was embarrassed. Damn straight.

"Your letter of apology was nice. And the check you sent my parents more than covered the cost of the wedding. Obviously, we were too young, and not getting married was for the best. No hard feelings."

"I would like to explain. Or at least try." He pushed a hand through his hair, making a mess of it. "I know it was unforgivable what I did but—"

"Peter," she interrupted him, "I don't believe in dwelling on past mistakes. My life has turned out fine. I'm happy. Shall we go?"

He looked confused, even a little offended. Ha! What had he expected? Tears and her heart held out for him to study the old scars? Forget it. Jabbing at old scars was likely to make them bleed again.

"Okay," he said and turned to the full-length mirror framed in a kaleidoscope of shards of mirror and crystal.

She turned away so she wouldn't have to watch Peter knot his tie. She didn't want to witness that much intimacy. Instead, she examined the room for the slightest flaw.

There were none.

Give top clothing designers a crack at interior decoration and it was amazing what they came up with. The king-size bed—like all the beds in the Hush guest rooms—sported the finest mattress money could buy, but the bed linens were unique to the Carnaby. Oh, and the designer had had fun there. Multicolored circles on the duvet and a lacy bedskirt gave a sense that the bed was dressed—and meant to be undressed. The circles were picked up in the carpet that Piper had had specially made to the designer's specs. The initial impression was playful, but it was an adult playtime that the decor evoked.

This was Kit's favorite of the designer penthouses—which was the reason she'd asked for it for the first fantasy weekend. The rose-colored double Jacuzzi tub in the middle of the room had a Stella McCartney-designed screen that could be pulled across for privacy, or mere coquettishness, and faced a tall window overlooking Madison Avenue. It was one-way glass, so no one could see inside the suite, but from in here it was easy to feel as though you were on display—which, according to Piper, was a powerful fantasy.

Since Kit had sent a room attendant up here a couple of hours ahead of when their guest had been scheduled to arrive, the fireplace was already crackling beside the tub, the champagne was on ice. She knew without looking that twin luxury bathrobes hung from hooks against the wall and that a basket of the best Italian soaps and lotions sat by the tub.

In most hotel suites, a living/receiving area would be the main room, with a bedroom or two opening off it. Not at Hush. In this suite, Piper had decreed that the bedroom should be the main room. Opening off this room was a full bathroom with an aromatherapy steam shower, another door led to an efficiency kitchen with an intimate dining area, and two other doors led to an office and a dressing room/lounge.

Peter's things were nowhere to be seen, so, neatnik that he was, he must have stowed them away in the dressing room.

If she talked to him, she didn't have to think about his things, or the air of relaxed sexuality that hung in this room like the scent of a favorite perfume.

"I'm looking forward to hearing about all the places you've been. You wrote to me from London, as I recall." She still remembered receiving that letter and steeling herself to read it—after she'd managed to tape all the pieces together. She never did find a couple of the bits she'd thrown around in a rage, so it sounded like a Dear Jane letter written by a kid flunking remedial English.

I am so ry I h t you.
I hop ne day you'll give me.

For a while, she'd make word jumbles of the pieces of paper, as though the letter were some kind of code puzzle and if she could crack it she could figure out what had gone wrong. Then she decided to stop wasting her time on failed love. Dwelling on the past was for historians and old people. Not for Kit, who had a career to build and a life to live. New York beckoned. No one knew her there, and in a city of over eight million, what was one more broken heart?

She might have tossed the letter, but she had kept up with Peter's career. She knew that he'd worked for an international marketing firm. After being based in their London office, he'd been transferred to Hong Kong, then Brazil and had just been hired by a good marketing firm in New York. Reading the business press was important in her job, so it wasn't as if she could help seeing his name the odd time.

"That's right. It will be great to catch up." He put a hand on her shoulder as he said it, a light, warm gesture that was gone before she could shrug it off. But she couldn't shrug off a surge of feelings too complex and contradictory to name.

"How do you like the hotel?" she asked as they left his room and walked toward the elevator. She was determined to keep things light and impersonal, to treat him the way she'd treat any hotel guest.

"It's fantastic," he said. "I couldn't believe Piper went into the family business, but when I saw this place, I knew it was perfect for her."

"Have you seen Piper since you moved to New York?" She knew darned well he hadn't. Piper would have told her.

"No, I haven't seen her," he confirmed.

"I'm sure you'll get a chance this weekend."

Light conversation kept them going until the elevator arrived with quiet promptness, as though it took the name of the hotel it serviced seriously.

In the dim elevator with its mirrored walls, Kit studied Peter surreptitiously. He seemed a nice-looking stranger. The kind of man she'd certainly give a second glance. He'd be twenty-seven now, and definitely all grown up. Living in exotic places, or maybe the responsibility of his job, had given him an air of sophistication that was admittedly sexy. She could pretend he was an attractive stranger—if only he didn't smell so bloody familiar.

He'd dumped her without a moment's hesitation, but three years later he remained faithful to his Polo for men?

"Did you choose my room?"

"Of course. I think it's the best suite in the hotel."

"I've never seen a suite so ideally designed for lovers," he said.

Her heart might have skipped a tiny beat when he looked at her significantly on the last word, but she reacted smoothly. "Yes. Piper Devon has a vision. This hotel is a sensual retreat in a crazy world. It's perfect for new lovers, old married couples or singles. Everyone gets pampered and maybe gets a chance to try something new."

The elevator indicated they were at the lobby. She led the way toward Amuse Bouche, then paused. "Would you like a drink at the bar before dinner?" She gestured to Erotique, adjacent to the restaurant.

"No, thanks. Maybe later."

She nodded and, after giving Dee, her favorite bartender, a discreet wave, she headed to the restaurant. "You are about to have your palate pampered. Our chef, Jacob Hill, is the hottest in the city. Piper lured him from L.A. and did New York a huge favor."

The dining room was full, which she'd expected, but still she breathed a tiny sigh of relief. With the *Times* coming, she wanted Amuse Bouche to appear hip, intimate and packed.

"Good evening, Ms. Prestcott. Mr. Garson," Walter, the maître d', said, never showing a hint of surprise that Kit herself was dining with their winner. Walter promptly led them to a table for two, which had the appearance of being nestled in a private alcove due to the clever use of screens. On the way, she waved to a couple of diners whom she knew would want to be recognized. There were two couples present who were the sort that didn't care to be seen or fussed over. To them, she was blind. Still, she scanned the room quickly to see that everything looked perfect.

It did, of course. The chef was as much of a perfectionist as she was herself.

"Well," she said when they were seated. "You have a choice. You can order anything off the menu or our amazing chef can surprise us."

He sent her a half grin and it stopped her cold. He'd been a good-looking guy in his mid-twenties, but three years later, he looked even better. She had a feeling he'd continue improving for a good while yet. "Maybe you've had enough surprises for one day."

"I love surprises. Speaking of which, wait until I give you the full tour of the hotel after dinner. I think you'll be impressed at all the innovations Piper's thought up. She is absolutely amazing."

"I'm sure she is."

"And this weekend you are going to be so pampered you won't know what hit you."

"As I recall, the contest said this weekend was about having anything I want."

"Within the law, of course," she said with a small laugh, hating the way she felt with his eyes resting on her so warmly.

"What I want is for you to drop the PR gal routine and talk to me."

Fortunately, the sommelier chose that moment to show up and they decided to sample the chef's tasting menu and let the sommelier pair the wines with each course. That was quick and easy, but it then left Kit without the prop of her menu to hide behind.

She decided to answer Peter's question. "Don't forget that the reason we're having dinner is because I'm the PR gal."

"Look, given the nature of our work, it's likely we'll bump into each other. It would be nice if we could be friends. That's why I wanted to see you again."

She blinked at him. Okay, she didn't believe for one second that his turning out to be the winner was a strange quirk of fate, but she'd decided to pretend she did. How dare he confront her with the fact that he'd manipulated her.

"You couldn't just call me?"

Two glasses of chilled white wine appeared in front of them along with a pair of tiny towers that included sea asparagus, morsels of lobster decorated with jewel-like caviar.

"Would you have seen me?"

She thought about it. "Probably not."

"Then here's to a new beginning," he said raising his glass in a toast.

She didn't raise her glass, or her voice, but she leaned forward and said, "Where do you get off thinking I would ever be interested in having you in my life again?"

He gazed at her with eyes as dark and mysterious as a lover's secrets. "You read my fantasy," he said. "And you chose me."

3

IF HE DIDN'T HAVE so much invested in the outcome of this evening, Peter would have laughed at the expression on Kit's face. Outrage, embarrassment and general pissiness were all mixed into an interesting shade of annoyed pink.

"I did not pick you for *me*," his date for the evening reminded him. "I chose your fantasy for its marketing potential, and don't forget it for a second."

"You're still angry with me."

"Really, you're not that important in my life."

Bickering was stupid. He didn't have much time to talk to Kit, and he didn't want to waste it on evasions so he jumped right into what he wanted to say to her. What he'd been wanting to say for the better part of three years. "Kit."

She raised her brows slightly. She was heart-stoppingly gorgeous. Her hair a much more sophisticated blond than the color he remembered, her face a little older and a lot sexier. "I can't believe I ran away like that."

"And you kept right on running. Did you think I was going to hunt you down and make you marry me? Honestly, you rated your own value way too high." She said it with a smile and the kind of inflection you'd give to a story that was leading to a funny punch line.

Okay, so maybe he had rated his own importance in her life a little highly. All this time he thought he'd broken her heart…

"What? You're looking at me like I'm speaking German."

"German I could understand. I learned it in Zurich." She rolled her gaze. "Figures."

Had he been slayed by guilt all this time for nothing? "Did I break your heart even a little bit?"

"Look, it's a great story. You dumped a girl on her wedding day. I don't want to spoil it for you. Really, it's a triumph few men can boast."

"I was an ass. Just tell me and get it over."

She leaned closer, giving him a tantalizing glimpse of smooth, pale skin and glossy lips he no longer had any right to kiss. "If you want absolution, go see a priest."

She popped the lobster off the top of her tiny food tower and into her mouth, then moaned with exaggerated pleasure as she chewed. She'd always thrown herself at life with gusto, whether trying new food or a new position in bed. He hadn't forgotten how pretty she was, but now that she was a little older, she was beautiful.

"Did you wait very long before you realized I wasn't coming?" Why was he pressing her like this? It was stupid and wasn't going to help make her forget what a bastard he'd been or convince her to let him back into her life even as a friend. But somehow he had to know. Maybe he hadn't seen Kit for three years, but he'd known her for a long time. She wasn't the type to go into therapy or counseling. He doubted she'd even cried on anyone's shoulder. She'd have rapidly decided it was all for the best, returned everyone's gifts, tossed her bridal dress and moved on.

She finished the rest of her first course with a sigh of satisfaction, took a sip of the white wine and then said, "About an hour. By then, Dad had already checked with the police that there hadn't been any car accidents in the area and with the hospital that they didn't have any amnesia patients wandering around in a tux with a white rose boutonniere."

He winced, feeling the pain she wouldn't show. "I never even saw your dress."

"Water under the bridge, honey." She raised her gaze and sent a delighted smile past his right shoulder. "I do believe I see scallops headed our way."

He was lying. He had seen Kit's wedding dress. Piper had sent him a letter that ought to have scorched out his eyeballs from reading it, and she'd included a photo of the bride in her dress and holding her bouquet. It was pretty obvious the girl in that photo had no notion she was about to be stood up. She looked...radiant. So sure of herself and her man, her eyes sparkling with excitement and so full of life you expected her to step right out of the snapshot. He had no idea why he still carried the thing in his wallet.

Her comment about absolution rang true, though. He suspected it was penance that had made him take this crazy step.

"Oh, well. You'll never see the dress now."

"You burned it?" he guessed.

She looked at him as if he were nuts. "You sure do love your drama, don't you. Of course I didn't burn the dress. I gave it to Nellie Redmond. She got pregnant in her third year and married that fellow Bert she'd been seeing. They didn't have much money, and she was close enough to my size."

She had given away her wedding dress. Of course she had. He bet she had even planned Nellie and Bert's wedding for them.

"What did you do? I mean, after you realized I wasn't coming that day?" They must have been on course seventeen. His bouche wasn't just amused, it was becoming bewildered.

"I got Piper to take charge of the reception. I changed into regular clothes, made an appearance, gave a speech that was pretty decent under the circumstances. I even managed to crack a few jokes. Then I left. I figured our guests would have a better time without me."

"That's it?"

"Well, I cried for a few days, but I was pretty busy, what with canceling the honeymoon and returning gifts. And then I decided that I was going to have to get on with my life. So I did."

He opened his mouth, but she shook her head. "Enough of the past. Tell me about your new job."

And so they chatted about his job, her job, and she caught him up on the fates of mutual acquaintances.

He knew each morsel was fabulous, but he kept forgetting to taste what he was eating as he knocked himself out to charm this woman he'd hurt so badly.

Not Kit. She raved about everything, even taking the trouble to ask the sommelier how he'd decided to choose a particular wine with one dish. She was like that, he remembered, always curious. And people talked to her, seemed flattered by her genuine interest. If she hadn't gone into PR, she'd have made a terrific journalist.

There was a minor flutter when some guy showed up with a camera, and Kit beamed when a TV crew showed up and an annoying young woman with spiked hair asked him personal questions. He did his best to sound thrilled about winning this fantasy weekend, for Kit's sake, and she quickly took over, feeding the reporter as many juicy little sound bites as he'd eaten courses.

As she kept things friendly but impersonal through the rest of the meal, he realized he had accomplished his goal. They were talking again. She laughed at his funny stories and asked intelligent questions about the places he'd lived. The door was open for them to be friends. He saw now how much he'd missed having her in his life.

Finally, the last taste of some lemony frothy dessert was gone, coffee finished and he felt his time with her was running out.

"So, are you seeing anyone?" he asked, wishing he hadn't even as the words emerged from his mouth.

She looked at him, her blue eyes chilling. "I see lots of people. Come on, let's tour the hotel." And she was back to PR gal mode so fast he barely caught up. She showed him private rooms for spontaneous fun and games, a spa so luxurious that even he, a card-carrying man's man, felt the urge for a pedicure, a library where he suspected more than just reading went on.

Although there was an undercurrent of eroticism everywhere, Piper had still managed to keep the feel elegant. Everything from the decor to the multitude of places a couple could hide away and indulge their passion got his own passion rising. As Kit walked ahead of him, her floaty skirt teasing him as it fluttered around her curves, he felt his body stir for her.

When they reached the door of his suite, she took a step back, letting him know there was no chance she was coming inside.

"Goodnight, Peter."

When she would have turned away, he suddenly grasped her shoulders forcing her to look up at him. "Why can't I move on?"

She blinked at him, stunned. "Huh?"

"I've dated women, lots of women since you."

"Thanks for sharing, but really I should be—"

"But it's no good. As soon as I even think about the future, I think this woman is too nice to get stuck with a bastard like me. What if I run out on her when she needs me?"

"That is not my problem."

"No. But you are part of it. I always end up thinking about you when I'm with another woman. Why is that?"

"Guilty conscience?"

He shook his head impatiently. "That's what I thought at first, too. Then I thought maybe I couldn't move on with my own life until I was sure that yours was okay."

"Then start moving, Peter. My life is more than okay. It's fantastic. I'm living out my dream. Thanks for realizing we were not a match and having the guts to act on it." She shook her had and laughed softly, "Can you imagine if we'd gone through with it? I would have hated getting divorced."

She was right. He should be pleased that she saw their breakup the same way he did. So why did her words feel like hail pellets raining down on his bare face?

She placed her palms either side of his jaw, rose to her tiptoes and kissed him softly. "Go on and have a wonderful life. I plan to."

She turned and walked away, and in that moment he knew exactly what his problem was.

If a lightning bolt had sizzled out of a blue sky and clocked him one, it couldn't have been more dazzlingly clear what his problem was.

He, Peter Garson, was still in love with Kirsten Prestcott.

And he had one weekend to figure out how the hell he was going to get her back.

4

Fantasy Weekend winner is in the Carnaby Suite.
Make sure he gets anything he wants! Refer all
media inquiries to Kit Prestcott.

Kit's finger hovered over the elevator buttons. The
hostess room she'd booked for Cassie was hers for the
night, and her things were in there. She kept a change
of outfit and toiletries at the hotel for the odd time she
worked so late that it would be crazy to travel across
town to her apartment. There were always spare rooms
in the hotel. Of course, when her PR mission was accomplished, that perk would end. She'd have to go home
to her own place no matter what, because there'd be
waiting lists every night for these rooms.

Right now, she felt too wired to sit alone in a hotel
room; besides, she had work to do. She had to find
someone to take her place tomorrow.

Her finger hovered over the panel and then hit the
button for the lobby. A few moments later, she was
walking into Erotique. Dee looked up from behind the
bar, glanced behind Kit's shoulder, and then, when she
realized Kit was alone, raised an eyebrow.

After taking a moment's professional pleasure in the fact that the restaurant was still almost full and the bar three quarters, even though it was midnight, Kit slid onto a stool as far away from other people as she could get.

Dee made her way down the bar, checking up on her customers until she arrived naturally in front of Kit.

"Where's the hunk o' burnin' love?" she asked. She had farmgirl-wholesome good looks that for some reason worked with the sleeveless pink tuxedo shirts the female bartenders wore.

"In his room."

"By himself? Now that is just a crime. Y'all looked like you were hitting it off when I saw you in the restaurant. He looked at you like you were a whole lot more interesting than what was on his plate."

"He's not my type," Kit said.

"I know. Tall, dark and handsome isn't my type, either," Dee said with a grin. "So, what are you doing here? You want a drink?"

"Do you have something that will put me to sleep and I won't wake up with a hangover?"

"Sure. Sleeping pills. What's with you? You seem jittery."

Kit stopped playing with her hair and put her hands in her lap. "I'll have a glass of white wine."

Dee shook her head. "Not with that dress."

Kit couldn't help but smile. Dee was the only bartender she knew who could make a drink a fashion accessory. "Oh, surprise me."

"I have exactly the thing. A blue sky martini." She poured a healthy dose of vodka and a much smaller amount of blue Curacao into a shaker and gave it a workout.

Kit asked, "Have you seen Piper tonight?"

"No. She and Trace went to bed early, I think." She shot a teasing grin at Kit. "They seem to do that a lot."

She'd been afraid of that. Of course, she was delighted that Piper had found such a great guy, but her friend and boss wasn't as available as she used to be. "I'll get hold of her in the morning, then. If you see her, let her know I'm looking."

Dee poured the drink into a martini glass and finished it with a twist of lemon. She placed the glass in front of Kit and squinted from the drink to her dress. "Not a bad match."

Kit sipped slowly. "Mmm. That's good."

"Much better than white wine. But the way you're acting, I think you'll need ten of them to put you to sleep."

"I really need to talk to Piper."

"Oh, wait a sec. I'm sure she said something about going to the Hamptons for the weekend. I just remembered."

Kit's eyes narrowed. "She never said anything to me."

"I got the feeling it was a sudden thing."

So much for the confrontation she'd been planning in her head. She drummed her freshly manicured fingertips against the bar's surface. She didn't believe for a second that Peter turning out to be her first fantasy winner was a coincidence. Piper and she had both gone to school with Peter, so it seemed pretty clear that Piper was the inside person on this con job to set her up with her ex. The question was why? Why would Piper play such a trick?

"Is there anything I can do?" Dee asked in the tone they must teach in bartending school. The open question that seemed to say, "Hey, if you want to talk about it, I'm here to listen, and if you don't want to talk about it, that's cool."

Not that Kit wanted to drag Dee into her troubles, but she figured a popular young bartender had to know a lot of people. "Maybe you can help me. I'm trying to find a hostess to finish out the weekend with our fantasy winner. You know a lot of people. Any ideas?"

Dee opened her eyes wide. "Are you out of your mind? That man is hot. Why would you give him away?"

She smiled tightly. "I was only filling in because Cassie didn't show up. I've got other things to do this weekend."

"Cancel them."

She dragged the pad of her index finger around the stem of the glass. "I used to know him. It's complicated."

She sipped her drink again, while Dee shook her head sadly. "I'd take on the job myself, but I'm working all weekend."

"I don't know what I'm going to do."

Dee leaned forward. "Do you want to see him again?"

"No."

"Then move your ass. He just got off the elevator."

With a tiny squeak of surprise and annoyance, she grabbed her clutch and hopped off the bar stool. "Thanks. I'll hide in the kitchen. Come and get me when he's gone."

"No time."

"Where?" Crazy to feel so panicked, but all she knew was she didn't want to see him, not now, and even more crazy to act so immature.

"He's coming this way. Go!"

Feeling like a panicked blue polka-dot butterfly, she

dashed to an empty table and, hoping everyone in the bar was too busy with their drinks or their companions to pay any notice, dropped to her knees and slithered under the table.

PETER FELT strangely restless—too wired to settle down, and he knew he was hours away from sleep. It wasn't every day you finally found the woman you loved and wanted to spend your life with. Too bad he hadn't had this revelation three years ago while he was still engaged to her.

A plan. He needed a plan.

This weekend was going to be critical if he wanted to get Kit back, and he had to make the most of every minute. Of course, Kit was going to try to blow him off.

Of course, he wasn't going to let her.

The sound of soft piano music spilled from the bar. He hadn't come down looking for a drink; he'd planned to head out of the hotel and walk for a while. But the place had a nice atmosphere, dark and intimate; even at this hour, it would be a lot quieter than the streets. So he decided on a nightcap.

As he walked in, he noticed the place was pretty full. Most of the booths were occupied—in one case by a couple who might want to take what they were doing upstairs. There were a few seats at the bar, so he slid into one—obviously just vacated since the bartender was removing a half-drunk blue cocktail. He could have sworn the seat was still warm when he sat down.

A memory of Kit as she'd been earlier that evening hit him with a keen sense of loneliness. They should be upstairs together, making love in every inch of that crazy sex palace, instead of him being down here alone. He breathed and realized her memory had been conjured by a trace of the scent she had been wearing earlier.

Her dress had been the color of that cocktail, he thought with a wry grin, knowing he had to have it bad if he was imagining her everywhere. But, wait a minute, there was a lipstick print on that glass. Same color as Kit's lips had been tonight.

Putting all the clues together, he didn't think he needed a detective's training to work out that Hush's PR expert had vacated this very seat. So recently, she'd left a trace of her perfume behind, and—based on the half-drunk cocktail—she'd left in a hurry.

He turned to scan the bar, but Kit was nowhere to be seen. She wasn't in the restaurant, either, unless she was hiding in the kitchen.

The bartender returned with a coaster that she placed in front of him. "What can I get you, sir?"

"A brandy. Thanks."

He waited until she'd returned with his drink to ask, "The lady who was sitting here before me, where did she go?"

The bartender glanced up quickly. "I didn't see her leave."

"Neither did I," he said pleasantly. "You'd think we'd have passed each other."

He got a professional smile in return. "Enjoying the hotel, sir?"

"Very much." He tried a charming grin on her. "I had a tour earlier. I liked all the places in the hotel you can... find privacy if you suddenly need it."

"Hush is great for that."

"Seems like every part of the hotel has a secret hide-away, or a few." He glanced around the bar again.

"Where would I go if I wanted privacy right here in Erotique?" he asked.

"It's pretty much what you see is what you get," she answered, but watching her closely he saw her glance rest on an empty table. It was dim in here, but not so dark he couldn't see there was nowhere to hide, unless…

"I guess there's enough room for two people under the table," he said, feeling better than he'd felt since Kit so calmly had walked away from him at the end of their tour.

If she was so freaked about seeing him again that she was hiding under the table, then her emotions were definitely engaged. Even if those emotions were negative ones.

"I've never spent much time under the tables. I wouldn't know," the bartender said. She sounded as if she wasn't sure whether to call security on him or hold his drink while he crawled under the table. Interesting.

"I tell you what, Dee," he said, reading her tag. "Why don't you pour me another brandy. I'm thinking that a curious guy like me ought to see if he can fit under the table."

"What are you going to do?" The bartender moved to pour the second drink, so he figured she was going to give him a chance, at least. She knew who was tucked under that table, and she knew that he knew.

"I'm going to offer a lady a nice quiet drink. After that? Well, I think I'll keep my options open."

She laughed, a strong sound that he liked. He had a feeling he and Dee were going to get along fine.

"Run a tab?" he asked her.

"It's on the house. This weekend? You can have pretty much anything you want."

"I hope you're right, Dee." He left her a ten-dollar tip, then picked up the two drinks.

Fortune favors the brave he reminded himself as he folded himself in half and peeked under the table.

He caught a flicker of flimsy blue fabric and dark polka dots. He crouched, bending his tall frame, and slid under to join her.

Kit turned her head and in the dim light her eyes glowed, mysterious and secret. "Here," he said, settling beside her and passing her a brandy. She sat with her back against the center support for the table, so he sat beside her with his knees up.

"Thanks."

"Looking for a lost earring?" he asked.

The look she sent him was neither embarrassed nor amused. "No."

"Ah. Hiding from someone?"

"More or less."

"I bet he's an ass."

"Oh, he can be." She sipped her drink and as he watched her he fell back in time. Why brandy? Why had he ordered brandy? In his student days he used to buy the stuff—and it wasn't the best—and he and Kit would share a glass after they'd made love sometimes. He'd had hundred-year-old Courvoisier and it had never tasted as good as the bar-brand stuff had tasted on her lips. Or her belly, or breasts, or any of the hundreds of places he'd dabbed it on her body and licked it off.

He sipped his own brandy. "I was looking for you."

"Here I am."

He kind of liked it down here. It felt sort of like a cave. There was music out there and dim lighting, people drinking, talking, laughing. All the hum and buzz in the lobby and coming off the street as guests returned from wherever they'd been to head up to bed. If they were staying in Hush, he doubted they were headed there for sleep.

Only he, the friggin' Fantasy Weekend Winner, was going to be tucked up solo in his sex palace for one. Oh, not if he could help it.

"I forgot to give you my list," he said.

"List?" Her voice sounded breathy and odd and he had the strangest notion she was afraid. When they were in public and she was doing the PR thing, she could hide behind her professional veneer, but now that he'd caught her hiding under the table, it was obvious she had strong feelings.

Unfortunately, they were feelings of aversion, but he figured anything was better than that kiss of death she'd given him earlier. That, and the thanks-for-breaking-up-with-me-and-doing-me-a-favor routine.

"The list of things I want to do tomorrow. I brought you my choices. I thought we'd start with the Met."

She rested her head back against the center support for the table, the way she'd rest against a tree trunk if they were on a picnic. "I still have to line up a hostess for you for the rest of the weekend. Once I do, I'll…" She turned and even in the dark under the table, her hair gleamed gold. "Did you say the Met?"

"That's right."

"As in, Metropolitan Museum?"

"That's right. And I don't want another woman. I want you."

"But that's not poss—"

"Anything I want. That's what I was promised. I want to spend Saturday with the same woman with whom I spent Friday night. You have a problem with that?"

"Yes. As a matter of fact I do." She whispered as though the people at the bar might be eavesdropping.

Her halter bodice thing was fluttering like moth wings. Her heart must be jumping all over itself. She twirled one blond curl around her finger. Was she so nervous to be here with him? What was she afraid of? That she'd fall apart if he touched her?

He wanted to touch her so badly his fingers burned.

She had her knees pulled up and the skirt draped around her. He reached out and wrapped a hand around her leg, just above her ankle. Her skin was soft and warm; when he touched her, she jumped so that her head hit the underside of the heavy wooden table.

"What are you doing?"

"Checking to see whether I make you nervous."

She stared at him and he stared back, so many unspoken messages zapped back and forth between them it was like a high-speed connection. It was close and intimate, and utterly ridiculous to sit under a table and want this woman with every atom of his being. But he did.

He didn't release her ankle, but he didn't try to move his hand, either.

"Give me your list," she whispered. "I'll get tomorrow organized."

He narrowed his eyes and leaned a little closer so she'd know he meant business. "And you'll be my hostess?"

"Like you said, anything the customer wants." She glared at him, "Except—"

"I know," he interrupted. "Except maybe this," and he leaned all the way in and kissed her. Not hard, but soft. His eyes drifted shut as he leaned into her, tasting the oh-so-painfully-familiar flavor of brandy on her lips.

Kit didn't pull away or hit him or do much of anything. She remained motionless, as though she couldn't make up her mind whether to respond or not. If there was one thing he'd learned about women, it was patience. So he didn't push, but he didn't back away, either; he just kept moving his lips over hers until he felt her soften. Her mouth eased from prim as her lips slid apart to let him in. At that same moment, he felt the tense muscle of her calf ease under his hand.

He licked into her mouth and found it both familiar and brand-new. She was the woman he'd always known and run from loving, the soul mate he'd treated like a carelessly lost sock.

He wanted to tell her his revelation—that he loved her still, had always loved her. But if being this close to him made her nervous, a confession like that was going to have her running farther than he had. Kit tended to be a little competitive. When he'd panicked, he'd run to Asia. If she ran away from him, she was likely to book a rocket to Mars.

Then suddenly she was kissing him back and he felt the turboboost of lust roar through him. He ached for her, wanted to take her here and now, drag her up to his room and spend the entire weekend with the Do Not Disturb sign on the door.

Easy, easy, he reminded himself, even as he changed the angle to deepen the kiss. He put his glass on the carpet and followed the line of her arm until he found hers. He took it from her unresisting fingers and placed that on the ground, as well.

With her hands free, she pushed her fingers into his hair and kissed him with some of her old enthusiasm. Oh, this was good. The hand that had waited so patiently at her calf waited no longer, but tracked slowly up her leg. He hit her knees but she kept them locked tightly together, so he slid beneath and reached under the soft flutter of her dress for the smooth line of thigh. She sucked in her breath and he felt the struggle within her. She wanted him, and she didn't want to want him.

What had he expected? For all her spin-doctor take on the dramatic collapse of their relationship, he'd really hurt her. If he was going to regain her trust, he wouldn't do it by fooling around under a bar table.

But the skin of her thigh was smooth and warm and he could feel her heat, drawing him closer in spite of his better judgment.

Just once. He only had to touch her once. He promised himself that would be it. Her knees hadn't opened but she hadn't pushed him away, either, and her hands were burrowing under his shirt to reach skin. Whatever had been wrong between them, it had never been sex.

He let his fingers slide a little closer to the source of all that heat, and her struggle increased. Her hands were fisting on his back as though she were fighting her attraction. As her hands clenched, he felt her nails dig into his skin.

"Let go, baby. Let go," he whispered against her mouth.

"You bastard," she said, in a low, choked voice, even as her knees parted.

"I'm sorry," he whispered, "I wish I could go back."

He reached for her blindly, cupping her heat, feeling the fever of her desire even as he understood that she didn't want to feel this way.

"We can never go back," she whispered, even as she mimicked his action and cupped the source of his own fever.

Somebody had got the saying wrong, he realized. It wasn't love that was blind, but lust. Even as he wanted her with blind need, the fact that he loved her stopped him.

She was right. They couldn't go back.

But they could start over. At least, he hoped so.

A man didn't get the girl of his dreams by making out with her under a bar table. He got her—if all the songs, and movies and fairy tales were right—by wooing the hell out of her.

He let her touch him a little longer, prolonging his own torture, and he let himself hold on to her, resisting the urge to delve under her panties, knowing that would be the end of him. Instead, he ran his hand up the center of her body, trailed his fingers up the soft skin of her throat and cupped her jaw. He took the kiss down from incendiary to warm.

"Come up to my suite. The first time I make love with you, I'm going to need a lot more room and a whole lot more privacy."

She shook her head as though a bee were after her. "The first time was about six years ago. And it didn't end so well."

"This will be the first time for the new and improved us."

She snorted, but since he didn't want to have a stupid argument in their current position, he turned his back on her and crawled out from under the table. As he rose, he nearly bumped into an athletic-looking young guy and a girl who looked as if she had spent her formative years yelling things like, "Give me a *G!*"

Peter was aware that his shirt was hanging out of his pants, and he was seriously rumpled. Behind him, Kit crawled out looking sexy, mussed and pissed.

"Wow," said Jock Boy, bending down. "What's under there? We were just in Exhibit A." He jiggled his pelvis in the direction of his girlfriend, who giggled. "This place is sweet."

"You're right," Peter said. "That's what they call it under there. The Sweet Spot. Help yourself. We warmed it up for you."

Even as Kit said, "Peter," in a furious undertone, the sex-crazed jock and jockette were crawling under the table. Peter leaned down. "What do you want to drink? I'll put in your order at the bar."

5

"SHOPPING? HE WANTS to go shopping?" Kit shrieked as she paced up and down her hotel room, her cell glued to her ear and her ever-ready smile out of batteries.

"Honey, calm down," Piper said, her voice sounding altogether too content and unruffled for someone who'd just been woken at close to one in the morning. "I don't know what you're talking about. Also, you just interrupted some of the greatest sex of my life so I'm not at my best."

Oh, no wonder she sounded so pleased with herself. Great sex. Just what Kit did not want to think about right now, especially as she could be having some this very second if she made her way to the eighteenth floor. The image of that amazing room and her and Peter in it... Oh, don't go there. Besides, she was too mad to go there. Peter's list vibrated in her hand as she stomped across the plush carpet.

"Well, sorry to interrupt the great sex, but I hear you're off to the Hamptons early in the morning so I might not get another chance to talk to you."

"I think—"

"This is Peter Garson's idea of the perfect day," she interrupted, reading from the list that was quivering in her hand. "The Metropolitan Museum, followed by a picnic lunch in Central Park and then shopping. He wants to return here for spa services, then rush off to Broadway to see *Love Ya, Babe.*"

"It's nominated for a bunch of Tonys, and you've been dying to see that play."

She ground her teeth. "Exactly." And how the hell did Peter know that?

"What else is on the list?"

"Dinner on the roof patio. Dancing to follow."

Piper laughed, the husky sound of a woman who gets a lot of great sex with a man not currently driving her insane. "He's either turned gay or he's wooing you."

After their little tussle under the table, she didn't think he'd changed his sexual orientation. "That bastard is putting the moves on me. I know him. He would never choose all this stuff. It's my ideal day, not his. What the hell should I do?"

"Look, honey, when a man goes to all that trouble to do everything you love, you just have to punish him. Enjoy the museum. Make him spend hours in the costume galleries. Insist you both have fruit salad for lunch. Shop for dresses. Make him have a facial. Not only see that play but make him discuss how it makes him *feel* afterward." She chuckled, a low, evil laugh. "If he gets through all that, I really think you should forgive him."

"But he almost ruined my life."

"Okay. You're right. What was I thinking? Let's make it a strawberry facial. And a hot wax pedicure."

"You set me up for this, didn't you?"

There was a sigh.

Somehow this was one of the toughest parts of the fiasco. "You're supposed to be my friend."

"I am your friend. Always. Maybe I was wrong not to let you know Peter was the winner. I don't know. It felt to me as if you needed some closure on the whole broken engagement thing. Needed to at least have the chance to talk to the guy again and let him know what he did to you."

"But you set me up!"

There was a short pause. "Did I? We both read those entries. Seems to me he won fair and square. All I did was keep his name off his entry. He penned the fantasy, and I think it got to you."

"Yes. Well. Now I'm stuck with him for the whole weekend."

"Doing everything in the world you love. I am really having trouble feeling very sorry for you. Mmm," she made a sound that suggested Kit was losing her friend's attention. "Oh, Trace, stop it…"

"Well, I guess I'd better let you go, then." If there was one thing Kit did not want to do right now, it was overhear Piper and Trace going at it, which they were obviously about to do.

"Love you," Piper said, but whether she was speaking to Kit or to Trace it was impossible to tell, so she pressed End without another word.

She slumped to the bed and regarded the list one more time.

So, Peter Garson was wooing her, was he?

She glanced over each item again and had to agree; if he wasn't wooing her, he was sure sucking up to her for some reason.

What irked her so much about this?

She flopped back on the bed and stared at the ceiling. Piper was right, in a way. It had been nice to see

Peter again. It was good to know that he obviously felt badly about running away from their wedding. She supposed the fact that he was trying to get close to her was an apology of sorts.

The thing was, she hadn't lied. After the crush of heartbreak, she'd done more with her life than she ever would have if they'd married. She'd been free to focus on nothing but her career, and she was doing very well. Certainly she had a reputation for doing the outlandish and daring—and getting attention in the Manhattan media wasn't the easiest task in the world.

Okay, so she wasn't sorry to see Peter again. It was even convenient to think of having sex with the guy again. That foolishness in the bar had made it pretty clear to her that her body responded as it always had. Great. Then what was she doing up here by herself when a very attractive and sexy man had invited her to his room?

She was here, alone in a Hush bedroom—she realized—because it pissed her off to be so out of control. She was the organizer. *She* was the event planner. She didn't passively sit around and wait for men to ask her to their rooms. Here she was, nothing but a stand-in hostess, while Peter was giving her a list of things he wanted to do, and she had to trot along by his side like the chirpy Manhattan Welcome Wagon.

Welcome to the Metropolitan Museum, sir.

Welcome to Central Park, Mr. Garson.

Welcome to Hush, the ultimate in erotic boutique hotels, Peter.

From the moment Peter had opened the door of the Carnaby Suite, she'd been knocked off balance and out of control. And Kit didn't like that a bit.

What this relationship needed, she realized, was for her to take back the lead. Diving under tables when she saw the man was not her style.

She sat up in bed so fast she got dizzy. Some things couldn't be explained.

They had to be demonstrated.

She put a hand to her chest as she realized she knew the perfect way to send him that message.

Could she do what she had in mind?

Hell, yes.

She got up off the bed, found her briefcase and rummaged through it until she came to the file she was looking for. It was suitably bright red. She read through it, nodded once and called downstairs to the night manager. "The Boutique's closed, but I need to get in."

It was simple enough to arrange what she needed and she found that once she got started, nothing was going to stop her.

PETER FLIPPED stations with about as much enthusiasm as he'd give to, say, washing his car.

NBA basketball wasn't holding his attention.

How come the news was never good?

Porn stations—and Piper seemed to subscribe to every pervy station beamed by every satellite in space— couldn't hold his interest after he'd been so close to the real thing.

He should change rooms. They'd promised him anything he wanted, and right now he did not want to be shacking up solo in the most sensual suite he'd ever seen. It was pathetic.

Sure, he could stroll back downstairs and find someone warm and willing to share the amenities of the Carnaby Suite, but he didn't want someone.

He wanted Kit. He wanted her so badly his body ached and his blood pounded.

If she'd wanted to punish him for the past she couldn't have found a better way than to let him have a taste of her, then back off.

Not that he didn't deserve the punishment, but a big dose of remorse wasn't going to help him sleep in this frilly lady's boudoir of a bed, either.

The ice had all melted in the ice bucket by the mega Jacuzzi. He knew that the floor-to-ceiling windows were made of some special glass so no one could see inside, but somehow he felt exposed, as though everyone in the five boroughs could see into his room and observe him dateless in the sex palace. He hadn't even bothered to undress. All he'd taken off were his socks. He was like a guy who'd been transported from the office to a swanky hotel room by accident.

Oh, the hell with it. He'd pull out some work. If he wasn't going to sleep, he might as well do something useful.

Flicking off the TV, he dragged out his briefcase and propped himself on the frilly bed against the frilly pillows and spread out his files on the frilly spread and his laptop across his knees.

He'd been brought into the marketing firm as a vice president. The firm had a sound reputation and he'd been able to bring in some big international clients, but he also needed to pull in some New York companies. He'd set himself some targets, some gets that were fairly getable, in his opinion, and some pie-in-the-sky ones, simply to keep things interesting.

Everybody was after the big guys, obviously. He liked to work slowly, never stealing a client, but letting them see that his firm was a logical next step.

Looking out the window of this hotel, he saw the city laid out before him. He was going to make his way here. He'd worked hard to earn the right. He didn't intend to blow it.

He was skimming a research report and making notes on his laptop when there was a knock at the door. He glanced at the bedside clock in the shape of Big Ben.

Turn down service at 2 a.m.? He didn't think so.

Even as he told himself to be cool and tried to prepare himself for some sex-starved idiot who'd got the wrong room, hope leapt inside him. He put aside his laptop and padded barefoot to the door.

If his gut had leapt at the sound of the knock, something else leapt when he saw the woman standing outside.

Her blond, sleek hair was in one of those society woman bun things. Her black dress revealed nothing, and hinted at everything. It came to just above her knee, showcasing her fantastic legs. She wore sheer black stockings and high, high shiny black heels. There were pearls around her neck. A long string of elegant pearls.

Kit's makeup was the same as earlier, except she'd done something to her mouth. He didn't know they made lipstick that red. Or that glossy.

"May I come in?" she asked, crisp and cool.

Where was the woman who'd hidden under the bar table rather than face him? Where was the woman who'd rejected his advances?

She sure as hell wasn't staring at him from that cool, ice-princess gaze.

Unable to speak, he opened the door wider and stood back.

She swept in, and nothing could stop him staring at the way her hips swayed in that prim but not prim dress. She stopped and surveyed the room for a moment, then disappeared into the other room. It was a kind of office. What was she doing?

She emerged carrying the upright chair from the desk. She hauled it over to the dark window, then turned it so it faced into the room.

She pointed, without saying a word.

Only now did he get it.

His fantasy.

For a second, he hesitated. When he'd written the thing he'd been concentrating on how to appeal to Kit, what would make her choose him. A fantasy was fun on paper, or whispered together in the dark, but did he want to play this one out?

He wasn't at all sure he did.

It seemed she didn't care.

When he didn't immediately move, her brows rose in silent challenge. He got the feeling if he didn't scoot his ass into that chair right quick, he'd be watching hers sashay out the door.

He walked over to the chair. He sat.

Felt the wool of his slacks pull tight across the ridge of his erection and figured what the hell. Maybe he did want to play this game.

She walked over to the console and pushed some buttons and two things happened. The lights dimmed and music came on. Soft, sultry music with a Latin beat. He remained seated. Somehow, he didn't think she was going to ask him to dance.

Instead, she ignored him. She walked—no, that was not walking, that was strutting and the old Kit Prestcott wouldn't have had it in her to strut like that. It made him wonder about what she'd been doing with herself for the last three years. Not that he had any right to ask, but it made him wonder all the same.

So she strutted until she was in front of a mirror. She raised her hands to the zip at the back of her dress and their eyes caught in the reflection and held. Oh, she'd placed his chair at the exact spot so he had a clear view of her in the mirror and her in the flesh. Okay, so she'd read his fantasy, and this was his fantasy weekend, so she was going to act it out for him.

Why did he suspect she wasn't going to go entirely by the script?

Not that he was going to stop her. Not when her fingers latched on to the zipper and she pulled so slowly he could feel each zipper tooth catch and try to hang on before losing its grip. A little like the way he was feeling right this second.

Mesmerized, he watched as each little tooth opened wide extending the vee. She had her head tilted slightly forward to keep her hair out of the zipper and as the dress fabric parted, and more of her white skin appeared he found himself getting goose bumps everywhere. And sitting still was as much of a trial as he'd imagined it would be when he had penned that absurd fantasy.

Did she know how much she was getting to him already?

Her eyes did a slow cruise up and down his body, and then a tiny smile tilted her lips. Oh, yeah. She knew.

And still the zipper tracked down her back as though she had all night. It wasn't a striptease, exactly. It was more like watching a woman undressing—as though he were watching her through a window. She knew he was there, but she was in her own space and—so long as he played by the rules and remained on his chair—he was very much in his.

A lacy black strap was revealed, stretching across her upper back. It hit him harder than full frontal nudity. She was all tease and suggestion, as his penned fantasy had been. She got that. Got how erotic it was.

A little lower. The dress sagged against the curve of her hip and he wanted to put his hand there so badly his palm tingled. The panty wasn't the thong he'd half expected, but a see-through gauzy affair that shadowed the curves of her ass. She turned, holding the dress up to her chin, so now it was her back in the mirror and he was watching her front.

He waited for her to taunt him; he imagined her sliding the dress down inch after inch, but once again she surprised him. She let go and the thing slid down her body like a lover's caress. He could have sworn he heard the hush of the material slipping against her skin.

Gazing at him from under her lashes, she stepped out of the dress, leaving it on the floor, and moved toward him. Her breasts were full and firm, teasing him, tantalizing him. Had she always been this sexy or had she grown into her sexuality? He remembered her as fun in bed, always eager to explore new things, compensating in enthusiasm for what she lacked in technique. But this, he reminded himself, wasn't her idea. The strip show was his.

If the underwear wasn't as all out stripper-gaudy as he'd imagined in his fantasy, this see-through black silk was every inch as erotic. Her nipples looked like copper pennies beneath the sheer black silk bra. Her panties didn't hide, but hinted at her secrets, and she wore a classy satin garter belt. He loved the few inches of white thigh that rode above the stocking tops. She looked like sex in heels.

When she got close to him, she turned and struck a pose, so he saw the long, lean line of her from the side view. She tilted her head back so her neck was a slim, arching line that would make an artist weep. Her hands rose and went to the back of her head. The muscles pulled her breasts taut and up so they were displayed in perfect silhouette. How much longer did she think he could sit here and do nothing but watch?

In an instant, she'd undone her hair so it swished down in perfect shampoo-commercial splendor. She shook her head a few times and the golden strands floated like silk to settle around her shoulders. Only now did she complete her journey over to him.

He didn't dare say a word, so afraid was he to break the spell. She reached down and pulled a neatly folded piece of white paper lodged in the top of her stocking.

As she unfolded it, he saw that it was a computer printout.

She took the two steps that would bring her to his side and leaned over. He could smell her scent, that same scent she'd worn earlier, but beneath it he smelled something earthy and feminine.

She placed her lips so close to his ear that he felt her breath, and read in a voice that was soft and smooth:

I can barely stay on my chair. I wish she'd tied me there so I wouldn't have to control myself, but she hasn't. She stops me with a glance. I can see her, smell her, and it's killing me not to touch her, taste her, take her.

6

"DO YOU RECOGNIZE those words?" she asked, still in that soft, teasing tone.

"Ye—" She stopped him with a finger to his lips. He swallowed. Nodded his head.

"You wrote those words." She shifted and he felt the warmth coming off her skin. "Do you remember what you wrote next?"

He nodded again. But she read his words anyway. He could tell they were turning her on as much as they aroused him.

She's close to naked, but still wearing that sexy underwear when she comes closer and straddles my lap.

He watched her move, stand in front of him for a moment, so confident and sexy, her legs parted, looming above him like a dominatrix. But instead of a whip in her hands, she brandished the words he'd written.

Catching his gaze and holding it, she straddled him. He felt her weight pressing on his thighs, felt the heat of her and, in spite of her cool demeanor, he felt the slight trembling in her body. She leaned forward, let her hair sweep across his face in a blond curtain as she once more put her lips against his ear.

Yes, I think. Finally. She undoes my tie, slips it out of my collar and then before I know what she's got in mind, she's putting it over my eyes and tying it behind my head.

When he'd written the stupid fantasy, he'd never envisioned acting it out. He'd wanted to catch Kit's attention, create a fantasy that was both erotic and tasteful, the way he assumed Piper's hotel would be. Never had he dreamed Kit would be straddling him on a hotel chair. The scent of her and the feel of her were all so familiar and yet so new. He felt her hair brush him as she moved so they were face-to-face, almost but not quite close enough to kiss.

She reached for his tie, which he'd foolishly left hanging open over his shirt, teasing him with it as she slipped it off. He tried to protest, looked as eagerly at her body as if he were a desert traveler gulping water at an oasis before being dragged away.

Then his world went dark as she tied the cool, slippery fabric of his own tie over his eyes.

Without his sight, all his other senses intensified. He felt her thighs, pressing warmly against his, heard her quick, shallow breathing, smelled her skin and her woman's scent.

"No," I say. I want to see her, but she only laughs, then she takes my hands and lets me touch her. She lets me take off her bra, and it's killing me because I can't see her. I feel as if I've known this woman forever, and that I've never met her. I touch her skin and feel the heat coming off her, I touch her intimate places, and know she wants me.

Will she let me love her? I don't know. I'm in agony, but it's up to her.

Those final words echoed in the air around him. In the darkness behind his blindfold he couldn't read the expression in her face or eyes. Would she let him love her or would she torture him?

"Kit, I—"

"Touch me," she whispered.

He didn't have to be asked twice.

He reached first for her breasts, because he couldn't help himself. When he touched them, she sighed. He traced the shape of them through the silk, loving the textures, the way his fingertips made a shushing noise as he rubbed her nipples. She drew her breath in sharply as the flesh pebbled against his fingertips.

She shifted and he felt her hair slide across his face as she leaned even closer. He could smell the scent of her thick lip gloss, and that made him picture her lushly painted mouth as she whispered, "What will happen next?"

He heard the crackling of paper. "Will she let me love her?" Her voice was low, sexy, as though considering the question. "I don't know. It's killing me. It will be up to her. Her choice. Her decision. She's in control." He heard his own words, realized she'd added a few of her own and that he'd had no idea when he originally penned his fantasy how much he would hate giving up control. Especially to a woman with a legitimate ax to grind.

He hadn't realized how intense his need would be, with the woman he was in love with—the woman he now realized he'd loved for years—splayed across his lap. What he couldn't see, he could imagine. The black silk panties would be pulled taut against her body, and he'd have teasing glimpses of her secrets.

She kissed him, and since he hadn't seen it coming, the shock of her lips, glossy and sticky against his, was like his first kiss ever. He leaned into it, into her, and she leaned back. He had the clasp open on her bra and her gorgeous breasts spilled into his eager hands.

Hers were busy getting him out of his shirt.

She ran her hands over his bare chest, his belly, then attacked his belt and zipper even as he reached to rub her through her silk panties.

She hissed in her breath as he touched her, feeling the heat pulsing from her. Too eager for finesse, he plunged his hand into her panties, needing to feel her, soft and slick and ready.

"Let me," he gasped. "Let me love you."

"Yes."

There was no way the chair could hold them, what with him trying to get her panties off at the same time she was trying to get his trousers. They tumbled off and onto the floor—the plush, deeply carpeted, made-for-rolling-around-having-wild-sex floor.

"I really, really need to see you," he said.

She kissed him again, rolling on top of him and straddling him. She didn't answer for a long moment and he tried to see himself from her vantage point, on the floor, mostly naked, with his own tie around his eyes. He felt her gaze on him. Knew he could simply rip off the tie and be done with it, but he also knew that she needed to be in control this first time, and he needed to give her that. So he waited, gazing sightlessly up at her.

"I guess I made my point," she said, and to his great relief, reached behind him and removed his blindfold.

He blinked, and blinked again as the fuzzy, pink-tinged image focused and it was Kit beside him on the floor, all pink and cream skin, with the black stockings and heels spicing things up.

"Oh, you are so beautiful," he said, gazing up at her.

"Don't move," she said, and ran to the bedside table, where Hush naturally stocked a variety of condoms. He watched her, reminding himself of all the parts of her body he liked so much. The round ass, the thighs she always complained were too big, but that he thought were muscular and sexy, especially when they gripped him.

The line of her back, and the delicate bones of her shoulders.

Breasts, belly, hips—all of her in her various parts that added up to such an amazing package.

She returned with a couple of foil squares, ripped one open with her teeth and sheathed him with her own hands. She took her time about it, sneaking in a caress or two, as though she was enjoying learning his body again as much as he was enjoying relearning hers. Letting her keep control, he stayed where he was on his back, feeling the soft wool of the carpet rubbing his spine.

She straddled him slowly and he watched intently as she gripped him in her hand and guided him to the entrance to her body. He barely breathed as she lowered herself slowly onto him, inching him slowly into heaven.

When she'd settled all the way, and he was as deep inside her as he could go, he gripped her hips, holding her against him so he could savor that first moment of complete connection.

He felt her heat, her snug, wet heat and the connection running between them that was so much more than physical. Their gazes caught and held, and he saw a flash of vulnerability. Something pulled deep inside him as he realized that he hadn't ever connected so deeply with anyone. Ever.

And then she closed her eyes against him. He felt a slight shudder run through her body, and then she was moving on him. He caught her rhythm and stayed with her, touching her as she rode him, touching her everywhere, her breasts, her hips, and, when he saw her eyes start to lose their focus, he touched her clit, rubbing it the way he remembered she liked it. When her head fell back on a cry, he thrust up, up and up inside her, pushing her over the edge, and then following in a great roaring rush.

Mmm, Kit thought as she lay slumped on top of Peter, feeling his heart thud beneath her breast. Just *mmm*. There was lots more that she could think, but anything more than a contemplation of her current state of physical well-being seemed like a dangerous idea.

Peter drew idle patterns on her back with his fingertips and she let herself enjoy the sensation and the utter relaxation in her body at this moment.

"That wasn't bad," he mumbled against her hair.

"Not bad?" She raised her head to glare down at him.

He grinned slowly, the tilt of his mouth widening slowly until he was beaming up at her. "Not bad for round one."

The relaxation that had enveloped her a moment past was gone as a familiar tension in her lower body built again.

"And this time," he said, rising to his feet and taking her hand, "I want to try that big fancy bed."

Oh, why not? Once was definitely not enough of something both so delicious and so addictive. It had been—how long? She tried to remember. Six months at least since she'd had sex, and that really hadn't been anything to get too excited about.

She felt as if she'd taken back control of this weekend rather definitely. By being the one to instigate sex, she felt she was calling the shots, and that was important to her with this man. Now she could be generous enough to let him take over round two. Which he did by placing her on her back, leaning over her and kissing her slowly.

He kissed her as though they were sharing their first kiss. He touched her lips gently with his own, moving his mouth over hers, warming her lips before touching her tongue lightly with his own. His restraint and sweetness charmed her, and she followed his lead, licking at him slowly, kissing as though they weren't going any farther than a kiss.

Oh, she'd forgotten how kissing could turn her on. Soon, the restless energy was pulsing through her. She wanted more. More of his mouth, more of his body, more of the friction that would send her flying.

Her breathing grew heavy, her body restless, and still he kissed only her mouth in that soft, teasing way. After seven eternities, he kissed his way to her breasts, kissing the slopes, the undersides and finally the sensitive tips. His tongue flicked over a nipple and she felt the charge right to her toes. While his mouth was busy at her breasts, his hands stroked her sides, her belly, her thighs and then settled between her legs.

He followed the path of his hands with his mouth until he was settled between her parted legs and his mouth hovered over her. His moist breath stirred her curls. The thought darted through her head that she should stop him—she'd taste like latex—then she remembered that Piper had thought of everything. The condoms were all fruit-flavored.

Then she didn't think anything at all because he put his mouth on her and put the same slow, restrained patience into licking her as he'd put into kissing her.

With the first rush of passion spent, she could enjoy a slower build, feel the pressure and moisture of his tongue, the way he explored even as he excited her. She built slowly, and then faster, until her hips were gyrating and her hands fisting against his shoulders.

So close.

He moved up her body and she would have begged him to take her if she didn't feel him already there, not so lazy now, not so slow. But he still took the time to look deep into her eyes when he entered her slowly and completely.

Lust, passion, memory—it all came together in a kind of bittersweet pleasure as he moved inside her. His palms cupped her face and he kissed her over and over again, even as their breaths grew ragged.

She tasted herself and a hint of cherry on his lips. And then she tasted him: hot, intense, fully aroused male. He tried to gaze into her eyes as she came but she wouldn't give him that intimacy, so she shut her eyes, wrapped her legs around him and gripped the firm muscles of his butt, kneading, pulling him deeper, grinding up to meet him.

As though a leash had snapped, he let himself go, bucking wildly against her until she shattered. It was the cue he'd waited for. Before her own cries had quieted, she heard him cry out his own release.

How could he be both so mysterious and so familiar, she wondered, as he rolled to his back, bringing her with him so she ended up snuggled against him, her head pillowed on his chest.

The sex was hauntingly familiar and yet so very different. The pull was still there, she admitted, as strong as ever, but now she knew that just because two people had amazing physical chemistry, it didn't mean they were soul mates.

How naive she'd been.

Good thing she was older and smarter. Now she could enjoy Peter's body and all the ways he knew how to please her without being in any danger of making a fool of herself a second time.

It seemed she was going to enjoy a fantasy weekend, too. When she'd planned to marry Peter, there had been a permanence in everything they did. She'd snuggle up to his warm body and think about kids and where they'd live, how she'd decorate their bedroom. Planning, she was always planning.

These days, her fantasy included making a stellar success of her career, enjoying life to the fullest and avoiding any entanglements that would impede the first two.

Now, she could focus on nothing but her body's pleasure with a man who physically excited her and with no concerns at all that he'd try to entangle her. It seemed she was enjoying a fantasy weekend, too.

PEOPLE HAD various notions about time travel—whether it was possible, and if so, how it was accomplished. Peter now knew that time travel was possible, and that for him, the portal to the past was making love with Kit.

He'd gone back in time. If he opened his eyes he'd

see Kit's school class schedule hanging on the wall. It had been one of those plastic permanent calendars and each class had been brightly labeled in a different colored marker, with her homework neatly penned beneath. He smiled at the recollection. She'd put math in black ink because it was her most loathed subject. Communications—her favorite—was in purple.

And yet, even as he fell back in time, he was also acutely in the present. She was wearing some light, sexy scent that was new, and he felt that he was different, more mature, old enough to appreciate what he'd so carelessly let go.

Was he any closer to getting her back now that they were so physically intimate? For all that their bodies had joined as spectacularly as ever, he felt, from the moment he'd seen that flash of vulnerability in her eyes, that she'd quickly hidden from him, that part of her was shut off. Maybe he wouldn't have noticed if he couldn't compare this Kit with the Kit of three years ago who'd been so open she never held anything back—not what she was thinking, or feeling, or what she wanted. Nor was she ever shy to ask him what he wanted.

Almost too open, he'd thought at the time. He wasn't used to it—not quite sure what to do with anyone who showed so much energy for everything from arguing politics to Friday night volleyball to lovemaking. It had made him a little uncomfortable, as though he were secretive when he was really just being his normal self.

And, of course, now that she'd become guarded— like most adults who'd been scarred a few times—and she wasn't putting it all out there, now that he wasn't party to every thought she had the second she had it, every wild idea that she'd turn into reality if he gave her the slightest encouragement, he found he missed it.

He wandered alone down memory lane and then suddenly laughed aloud.

"What?" Kit asked beside him.

"Do you remember when you made us all dress up and go to some fancy do at the yacht club? It was for members only, but you were trying to interview some tycoon or other for a course you were taking. You and me and Piper and some guy she had on the string, we all dressed up and tried to talk our way into the yacht club. They would have tossed us out if you hadn't been so convincing."

She didn't laugh along with him and he turned his head to see her smile perfunctorily. "That was a long time ago."

"It was a good time, Kit."

The possibility hovered in the air that she might actually let this conversation happen. For a second time, he caught sight of the vulnerability, he read the *why* in her eyes, and then it was gone. She rolled to the side of the bed and was on her feet before he could put out a hand to stop her.

He didn't say anything, in case she was going to the bathroom, but when she started dressing, he said, "Where are you going?"

The bright smile she sent him was as phony as the Smiley Face on her watch. "I've got a million things to organize for tomorrow. Have to keep the big winner in the Carnaby Suite happy, you know."

"You just made the guy in the Carnaby Suite incredibly happy. I'd be even happier if you stayed the night."

The second time they'd made love had been slow and

sweet, the kind of sex that ends in sleep. Except that he'd blown it by bringing up the past.

He stacked his hands behind his head and watched her.

Considering how long it had taken her to remove those clothes, she had them back on again in a heartbeat. He didn't know a woman could dress that fast. She walked around the bed and leaned in to kiss him quickly, all efficiency. The intimacy they'd shared was gone.

"I'll see you in the morning."

He watched her all the way to the door, and when she left, with a cheery wave that made him feel dismissed and, frankly, pissed-off he wondered if there was a lonelier place in the world than an entire suite designed for sex when the woman you loved and wanted to make love to was walking out the door.

Okay, she'd played this scene her way.

The next time they got naked, he decided, he'd be the one calling the shots. And her leaving right after doing the deed was not going to happen.

7

THERE WAS SHOPPING, and there was shopping.

There was Richard Gere taking Julia Roberts down Rodeo Drive and giving her carte blanche on his credit card in *Pretty Woman*.

That was romantic, sexy, and obviously the kind of shopping Peter had in mind—though she certainly wasn't interested in using his card. She had plenty of her own.

Then there was the kind of shopping every man she'd ever known—including Peter—loathed.

Kit allowed herself a small, satisfied smile as she glanced over the list she'd made.

Peter's punishment was about to begin.

He hadn't said anything about breakfast and she hadn't pried. After too few hours of sleep, she'd made do with a cup of coffee and a muffin in her office while she confirmed everything for the day.

Then she ran home to her own place for some clothes. Instead of picking him up in his room—which, after last night, was probably a bad idea—she called him from the lobby and had him meet her there.

He arrived in some kind of tweedy wool pants and a casual jacket. Totally Richard Gere in *Pretty Woman*. She wore jeans, a soft pink wrap-around shirt and the comfiest sneakers she owned.

When he walked toward her, her mind flashed to the night before when he'd first entered her body and she'd wanted to prove she could enjoy him for sex without the dangerous tangle of emotions. For about five seconds, she'd fooled herself it could be done. Then she'd wanted to weep. Or hit him. Both, maybe.

But the first time was bound to involve painful recollections, she reminded herself. He was still sexy and attractive to her. He'd won his fantasy weekend and she intended that he would have exactly that.

If she got some very nice sex out of the bargain, what was so terrible about that?

And if she made him suffer a teensy bit, well, she was only human.

"You really want to go shopping?" she asked, feeling suddenly guilty and giving him a last chance to back out.

"Absolutely," he said, not fooling her for a second.

"Great. Do you have anything you need to get?"

"Not really."

"Because I do." She pulled out a list that should have made him run screaming. "We could use the hotel limo if you want, but I thought it might be more fun to walk."

"Sure."

"The limo will pick us up and take us for lunch."

"We're going to Central Park in a limo?" Peter's steps faltered as they hadn't when he saw her long shopping list.

"That's right. You'll feel like a movie star or an oil sheikh."

"That's what I'm afraid of," he mumbled. But since they were passing out of the hotel as he spoke, she pretended she hadn't heard him over the sudden noise of traffic.

"Thanks, Carl," she said to today's cute doorman. She was certain they had the cutest doormen in all Manhattan.

"You're welcome, Kit. Can I call your limo?" He lifted his silver whistle as he spoke, but she shook her head. "We're going to walk."

"Okay. You have a nice day."

While they walked, she consulted her list. "I need to get a gift for my mother's birthday, I need some new place mats for my apartment, and I need a shower gift for Beck Desmond and May."

"Beck Desmond, the writer?"

"Yes. He's getting married to May, who came here as a guest and now does the flowers."

"Cool."

Peter leaned over her shoulder and she heard him chuckle.

"What?"

"Your list is in different colors."

"I know it's—"

"Don't tell me. I can guess," he said, his voice warm and filled with gentle humor. "You love your mom, so she got pink. Place mats are boring, so you wrote that in blue pen. I'm guessing you're excited about the wedding shower, because that's in purple."

She tucked the list away, realizing that Peter knew her far too well. This was a dangerous game she was playing. Sure, she was over him and the past was the past, but if he broke her heart again she didn't think she'd recover.

So they'd had some laughs, enjoyed some nice sex last night. It didn't mean she had to let herself get gushy over him. In trying to prove to everyone, especially Peter, that she was over him, she'd better make sure she stayed that way.

She kept the pace brisk. With the crowds and the noise of traffic, street vendors hawking their wares, sirens and cell phones, there wasn't much chance of conversation.

She swept through the revolving doors of Bloomingdale's with Peter gamely in pursuit. She'd been so busy making sure Peter got bored that she hadn't considered how weird it would be to shop for a bridal shower gift with a man she'd almost married.

Not a good idea. Maybe she'd leave the shower gift for later when she was on her own.

Place mats. Also on her list. But even buying something for her apartment with Peter was too intimate. Putting her food on place mats that he'd helped pick out? Scratch place mats off her list.

That left a gift for her mother.

"You know," she said, hesitating, "I think I'll get my mother something from the museum gift shop."

"Okay. But what about all that other stuff on your list?"

"Maybe later."

He shrugged. "Okay."

So she called the limo and they were whisked to the Metropolitan Museum of Art. As she went into one of her favorite places on Earth, she wondered why it had been so long since she'd been here.

"What's the matter?" Peter asked.

"Maybe I need to stop working so much. I haven't been here in almost a year. One of the reasons I moved to Manhattan was so I could go to Broadway and the Met and do all the things tourists dream of."

"So what happened?"

"I turned into a New Yorker. I never have time for any of that stuff anymore." She sighed. "It's a tragedy."

"Well, today you get to combine business and pleasure. What's not great about that?"

She narrowed her eyes at him. "How long have I got?"

"As long as you want."

She shook her head slowly. "You're not fooling me. How long until your feet start to hurt, you sit on the benches and play with your cell phone, and generally act like a pain in the ass?"

He gazed around the Great Hall that was currently filled with tourists and way too many parents who didn't believe in discipline. "An hour, tops."

Deciding not to take Piper's advice and drag him through the costumes galleries or worse, textiles, she tried to think what he'd most enjoy. "French Impressionists?" She raised her brows.

He looked marginally relieved. "Why not?"

Being a Saturday, the place was fairly crowded, but she sort of liked the ebb and flow of people. She didn't protest when Peter took her hand in his. He seemed happy to stop where she stopped, gaze at whatever caught her fancy. As they wandered around the second-floor galleries that displayed the Met's renowned collection of French and European paintings.

"She reminds me of you," he said after they went down the stairs to check out the modern-art galleries.

She followed his gaze. "The Modigliani, you mean?"

"Yes. The painting is called—" he stopped to read the sign "—Reclining Nude."

"I don't look a bit like her. She has that elongated face."

"Of course you don't look like her. But the pose, and the way she's so relaxed in her body, that's what you were like last night when you lay on that big bed with your arms over your head like that, and your head turned to look at me." He leaned closer. "I didn't know the Met was going to make me horny," he whispered.

She shook her head. "You are such a connoisseur of art."

"Hey," he said with a grin, "I know what I like."

"Let's go to the gift shop and get something for my mother."

"Okay. I wonder if they have posters of the Modigliani. My apartment's pretty bare."

"As a souvenir to remember this weekend?" she teased.

He stared at her and his look was so intimate she caught her breath. "I won't need any souvenirs to remember this weekend," he said. "And I'll never forget last night."

Her pulse jumped in a combination of unwilling response and alarm. "Peter, I—"

"So, how is your mom?" he asked, and she was glad he'd cut her off since she didn't know what to say.

"She's fine. Good."

"Are they still living in the same place?"

"Oh, yes."

When they got to the gift shop, Peter helped her choose a pair of silver-and-black onyx Parisian Art Deco earrings for her mother. That done, she realized it was time for lunch if they were going to stick to their schedule.

She loved having the limo at her disposal. The traffic nightmare that was New York was something she would never become accustomed to. She loved being chauffeured. And since she was on legitimate Hush business, she could indulge without feeling guilty.

"We're lucky it's still warm enough to picnic," she said as they sank back into the cushioned leather seats for the very short ride down Fifth Avenue and along East 72nd St. to the Bethesda Terrace in Central Park where the driver would let them out. From there, it was only a five-minute walk to Strawberry Fields, the perfect spot for a picnic.

"I was kind of hoping it would rain."

"You were?"

"Yes. Then we could have moved the picnic indoors."

"Where exactly, indoors?"

"My suite."

"Do you ever think of anything but sex?"

"Not this weekend," he said, and leaning forward kissed her softly.

When they reached the terrace, Big Al, the limo driver, unloaded a wicker picnic basket and a red plaid blanket from the trunk. When he would have carried it for them, Peter balked and insisted on taking over from there.

"We'll call you when we're done, Al. Thanks," Kit said as Peter took the basket.

"I was thinking of deli sandwiches in a paper bag," he muttered as he hauled along the basket.

They found a spot and kicked off their shoes. She spread the blanket and sank onto it. Peter settled beside her.

"I love it here," Kit said, tipping her face to the sun. Strawberry Fields, a two-and-half-acre, tear-shaped park, was designed in commemoration of John Lennon. A tribute to Lennon, a black-and-white mosaic, with the single word, *Imagine,* had become an unofficial shrine to his memory where fans left flowers and tokens. Today one white rose wilted in the heat.

They weren't the only ones picnicking in Strawberry Fields, but Kit suspected their meal was the most elegant.

She'd asked for something simple and rustic, but it was designer simple.

There was cold roast chicken with rosemary and lemon and artisan breads, cheeses and olives, grapes and apples and an almond and apple cake. There was Italian soda and sparkling water to drink and, to finish off, chocolate truffles.

"I feel like I should have brought a book of poetry and I should read it to you," Peter said as he demolished a chicken sandwich.

"What kind of poetry would you recite?" she asked him. The sun was warm on her face and the scent of grass and trees was a rare pleasure.

"I'd like to say it would be Shakespearean sonnets, but in truth?" he leaned over to touch her hair. "I'd read you erotic poetry."

Then Kit's cell phone rang, a mood shatterer if there ever was one. She checked the number. "Sorry," she said to Peter. "It's the hotel. I have to answer." Then she stuck her professional smile on her face and answered. "Kit Prestcott."

"We have a problem," said Janice, the hotel's general manager.

"What is it?"

"Our other fantasy winner checked in."

"Our other fantasy winner? But…there's only one."

"Irene Bonnet is standing at the registration desk at this very moment."

"Irene Bonnet?" Irene was the comedienne with the Cinderella fantasy. "She's the second winner. She's not due until next weekend."

"Well, the thing is—she's here."

"Look, call on all your tact, but she can't come this

weekend, she has to come next weekend. We already have a fantasy winner."

"She's waving around her congratulations letter—the one signed by Piper."

"Right."

"And the dates are for this weekend."

"No. That's impossible…"

"Kit, she's not the sort of person you can quietly fob off, if you know what I mean."

"Damn it, I should have proofed that letter myself before Piper signed it." She sucked in a breath.

"Why didn't she show up yesterday?"

"She said she had to perform somewhere on Friday night and she called Piper who told her she could change her Friday through Sunday to Saturday through Monday." Janice was putting on as much fake pleasantness as Kit, but it was clear she wanted to smack Piper right now as badly as Kit did.

"And Piper forgot to mention it to anyone."

"So it seems."

"The airhead gene raises its head again."

"I can't get hold of Piper to confirm."

"She's in the Hamptons. With Trace."

"Ah. Cell phone turned off."

"Yep."

"So, we're on our own."

"All right. This is not a disaster," she reminded them both, sitting up straighter and pushing her glass out of the way. The word *disaster* played like a drumbeat against the inside of her skull. *Disaster, disaster, disaster.*

Kit racked her brain to remember what the woman's fantasy was. She remembered that she and Piper had laughed. The woman had wanted to be a princess for one weekend. Piper thought every woman who stayed at Hush should feel like a princess. It was a nice marketing hook. "Are any of the suites free?"

"The Vera Wang and the Oscar de la Renta."

"Okay. Put her in the Oscar. It's more princessy. What's she like?"

There was a short pause. "She's unusual."

"Unusual in a good way? Like eccentric? Or unusual like somebody needs to go back on their meds?"

"Um. Kind of both. She's a stand-up comedienne. If you get my drift. I really think you need to get back here."

"All right. I'm sorry about this Janice, and thanks. I'll get her a host and we'll make this work. Don't worry."

Don't worry indeed. Why hadn't she gone into accounting like her dad had suggested?

She closed her phone and found Peter regarding her with a not-quite-disguised smirk. "Trouble?"

"Right here in River City. I've got a stand-up comedienne looking for a good time. Her letter had the wrong dates on it and she somehow got Piper involved who made a mess of the booking." She shook her head. "Piper's brilliant, but she's not a good detail person."

"I can imagine."

"Yeah. We never let her near the bookings."

"So, you've got a stand-up comic standing at Hush reception as we speak?"

Kit nodded. "And you know she's got to be looking for fresh material for her next gig."

"Don't you check these winners out before you choose them?"

She stared at him. "Obviously not. Look, can you go feed the ducks or something while I make some calls?

I'm sorry about this, but I've got to get a host for this woman, and fast."

She shook a warning finger at him. "And not one word about how that seems to be an epidemic. I am on to you."

He raised both hands in a peace gesture. "I wasn't going to say anything. Let me know if I can help."

"Unless you know the next Jerry Seinfeld, and he's single and lives in New York, then no."

Already she was scrolling through her stored numbers. The good news was that most of the people she'd already approached about being hosts or hostesses were in the entertainment business.

Roger was already organized for next week. Roger was a big teddy bear of a guy who'd been a bouncer and had briefly tried pro wrestling before settling in to work as a character actor. He'd had bit parts in *Law & Order*, *CSI: NY* and a couple of feature films. When he was waiting for the next part, he did a lot of partying. Roger had a great sense of humor. He'd seemed perfect. She called him and got his roommate. Apparently he was definitely partying this weekend.

In L.A.

It felt as if history was repeating itself as she went through exactly what she'd been through the day before, only this time it was male recorded voices telling her they weren't available, out of town, leave a message, blah, blah, blah. She left a couple of messages, but there wasn't time.

She was going to have to break her own rules and use one of the hotel staff to fill in—at least they had cute guys on call all weekend. It didn't feel right, though, and the last thing she wanted was to end up part of a stand-up routine that started, "Let me tell you about this door-man at Hush. Let's just say he didn't knock when he entered."

She started packing up the remains of the picnic without even seeing what she was doing.

"I take it you had no luck?"

"None."

Peter squatted beside her and helped her repack the basket, being a lot neater about it than she'd been.

"What is this woman's fantasy?"

"All I remember is that she had a princess fantasy. For a weekend, she wants to be pampered and treated like a princess. Now all I need is a handy Prince Charming, who happens to be sitting all alone in Manhattan on a Saturday afternoon." She dropped her forehead into her hand and groaned. "I am so screwed."

While a wave of panic threatened, Peter rubbed her back in friendly support.

"I have a friend," he said.

"Well, congratulations."

"No, I mean, he's a single man who is a great companion. A lot of fun, knows everyone. I know he's in town. He'd probably do me a favor if I asked him and spend some time with this woman."

"Can he show a loudmouthed woman who may or may not be funny around Manhattan?"

"Yes. That's what made me think of him. Giles is one of my clients, but I know he's in town this weekend, because he had an extra ticket to the, um, ballet this evening and he asked me if I wanted to go with him. If he hasn't found another taker, your princess gets to see *Swan Lake*."

She bit her lip, sorely tempted. "Is he anything like Prince Charming?"

Peter hesitated for a second and then said, "He's English."

"Really?" She stared at him. "Could there possibly be such a simple answer to our problem? Tell me more about this Giles. Is he good-looking at all?"

"I'm not the best person to ask, but I guess. He looks sort of like that guy who used to be on *Cheers*. The one that Kirstie Alley had the hots for."

"Roger Rees? He looks like Roger Rees?"

"Yeah. Kind of."

"Cool."

"And you think he'd do this?"

"I think he might."

"The pay's great for a struggling actor, but I'm not sure any client of yours is going to—"

"I think if you offered to make a nice donation to one of his charities, that would be great. Giles does very well for himself. He does not need the money."

She sat back on her heels. "It's nice of you, but I don't know. I mean, he's your client, and this is so not your problem."

"I'm not being nice. I'm being selfish. What kind of a hot weekend am I going to have if my fantasy lover is working 24/7?"

In spite of her stress level, she laughed. "Right now, my fantasy is that I'd taken my dad's advice and gone into accounting."

"Not me," he said, suddenly turning serious. "This weekend is…" He stared into her eyes and she saw a lot of things she didn't even want to think about. "Kit, I—"

She shook her head violently. "No. I can't talk about this now. Any more tension in this body and it's going to blow up."

"Hey," he said, taking her arm in a warm grip. "You'll pull this off. You always do."

Her eyelids fluttered shut and she let herself take strength from his warm fingers circling her arm. Oh, what the hell. Giles probably wouldn't be around anyway.

Without opening her eyes, or giving herself a chance for second thoughts, she shoved her phone at Peter. "Call him."

8

TWENTY-FOUR HOURS. That's all it had been. Twenty-four hours since she'd believed Peter was out of her life forever.

If, at this time yesterday, she'd had to make a list of men she trusted, Peter Garson's name most definitely would not have appeared.

And yet, here she was, barely a day later, trusting him to provide her with a weekend escort for one of the most important promotions of her career. Was she nuts?

Her heart was doing a lot of things in her chest that didn't seem healthy. Bumping and knocking and something that felt like the jitterbug. If she were attached to an electrocardiograph right now, she'd bet they'd slap her in the ICU faster than you could say "You're fired."

Peter, walking at her side into the lobby of Hush, gripped her shoulder. "Not to worry. You can trust me."

She glanced up at him. "I am trusting you. That is what's worrying me."

There wasn't time for more.

"Giles," Peter said, stepping forward with his hand out.

A tall, slender man rose from one of the comfy chairs in the lobby, meticulously folded *The Economist* and stepped forward.

He had dark hair that was perfectly groomed, with a

hint of gray that only made his thin, intellectual face more attractive. His light gray eyes held an amused expression. She would have said she couldn't pick out a Saville Row tailored suit, but somehow she knew she was looking at one.

"Peter," the man said, extending a well-manicured hand.

The men shook hands briefly. "Thanks for coming."

"I'm always happy to help an old friend out of a sticky situation. Besides," he said, looking around the lobby, "I've been curious about this place. Happy to have a chance to spend some time here."

"This is Kit Prestcott."

Kit held out her own hand and Giles shook it. "How do you do?" he said politely.

"We are so grateful to you for helping us out. Really."

"Pleasure, my dear. Now, do tell me, what exactly am I to do?"

"I don't want to be overheard," she said. "Would you mind coming to my office?"

"Not at all."

After first confirming that fantasy winner number two was happily ensconced in her room, and making sure Janice knew she was back on the premises, Kit escorted the two men to her office. Peter seemed more interested in the few personal belongings she had scattered around, and the citations and framed certificates and awards she had on the walls.

His friend Giles, she noted with relief, was as anxious to get down to discussing his role as she was.

"Before we get started, I need to explain the ground rules. Our winner can have anything she wants within reason, the law and what our hotel can provide. You are part of the prize package." She smiled, amazed at how perfect this guy was. "But the only thing we ask of you is that you escort your winner wherever she wants to go and try to keep her happy. You'll have a hotel room at your disposal, of course, and Hush will take care of all the expenses. Peter suggested you would rather have us make a donation to charity than give you the usual honorarium."

"Oh, yes. Absolutely."

"Fine. I'll arrange it."

She pulled out her red file of contest winners and found Irene's fantasy.

Before she placed it on the desk for them both to read, she said, "You realize this is confidential. You need to understand her fantasy, but you can't be too obvious about having read it."

"Naturally," Giles said, as though he shared women's secrets all the time.

"Okay," she said, and placed the single printed page on the desk.

What is my fantasy? No one's asked me that for a long time. Isn't that sad? I'm a woman. I might have a mouth bigger than the Holland Tunnel and an ass the size of Texas, but inside I'm still a young girl who wants to be swept off her feet by Prince Charming.

Or maybe I just want to be treated like a princess for a weekend. I want to eat the kind of food that makes you cry, it tastes so good, food that wipes away the taste of takeout that's pretty much ingrown in my tongue. I want to sleep on soft sheets, and wake up to find that the guy I went to bed with is still there. Even better if he still remembers my name.

My sexual fantasy is so bland I can't believe it's the best I can do, but, you know, I've tried pretty much everything, and I'm tired of pampering male egos and twisting myself up like an overweight pretzel. I think my fantasy is to lay back, close my eyes, and have some beautiful man take the time to pleasure me.

Oh, yeah. That's my fantasy.

Kit finished reading and suddenly felt hot and uncomfortable that she'd shared another woman's intimacies with this upper-class stranger.

"I should explain," she said, feeling embarrassed, "that you are under no obligation to, um…"

"That's quite all right. I understand what you mean." He glanced at the paper. "I thought her letter was funny and rather sweet. And, she sounds to me, rather lonely."

"Yes. I think she might also be a bit overweight. I hope you won't—"

"My dear. I promise you I will treat this woman like the princess she longs to be. As for the sexual—"

"No obligation. Really. The bedside tables are full of…fun toys for single people."

"You will not believe the stuff they stock in the bedside drawers," Peter interrupted. "She can lie back and get intimate with Mr. Rabbit."

Giles's black brows rose. "Ah. I had heard that Hush was a little out of the ordinary."

"We take pleasure seriously at this hotel. We try to make sure that everyone has a good time. Especially our fantasy winners."

"Did Peter tell you I've got tickets for the ballet?"

"Yes, he did mention it. It sounds perfect for our guest."

"I was able to get two more tickets. I'd love it if you and Peter would join us tonight."

"That would be wonderful. I love the ballet."

"But we're going to *Love Ya, Babe* tonight," Peter said, suddenly turning.

Kit had seen the appeal in Giles's eyes. What kind of a cruel person would she be to leave this poor, elegant man alone with a woman who admitted she had a big mouth?

"I can give the tickets away, Peter. It's not a problem. I'd love to see the ballet."

"I thought the play was going to be bad enough," Peter muttered, but she and Giles both pretended not to hear.

"Let's meet for drinks in Erotique at six?" Kit said.

"Perfect."

"In the meantime, I'll go find Irene and give her the hotel tour."

"But what about our afternoon in the spa?" Peter asked.

"Enjoy your treatments. It's one of the most self-indulgent afternoons you'll ever spend."

"Without you? I couldn't."

"Maybe Giles would like to take my place?" she said, glancing from one to the other. "I'm booked for a massage and a pedicure."

"Wonderful. I could rather do with a pedicure," he said, smiling blandly at Peter, who did not look thrilled with his change in spa partners.

She ushered the two men out of the office, promised to introduce Giles to his fantasy winner later that afternoon, and headed back to the lobby.

Once she had Giles checked in, he said, with a small

smile, "I'll see you in the spa then, Peter," and headed for the elevators.

"I don't want to go to *Swan Lake,* and I don't want a pedicure," Peter said in a furious undertone.

"Now, that's odd," she said, pulling out her list of his supposed preferred activities and scanning it. She nodded and pointed to his own handwriting on Hush letterhead. "Yep, there it is. Afternoon at the spa. Right between picnic in Central Park and the romantic comedy on Broadway." She smiled blandly at him. "At Hush, we aim to please."

"You know damn well I only picked those things because I thought you'd like them."

She stared at him for a moment. "If your fantasy is to make a fool of yourself, that's not my problem. Enjoy your pedicure."

"I never chose the ballet."

She was suddenly sorry she'd been so cranky. "I know. And it was so sweet of you to find Giles for me. He's perfect. But we can't abandon him to his date. We'll do the ballet and then have our dinner on the roof patio. Just the two of us."

Peter narrowed his eyes. "And afterward?"

She leaned up and kissed him lightly. "Anything the fantasy winner wants."

FIFTEEN MINUTES LATER, having thrown on a skirt and blouse, combed her hair and freshened her makeup, she was knocking on the door of the Oscar suite.

It was opened by a woman of around thirty-five, with multistreaked red hair in a short, sassy style, a slinky red top that showed impressive cleavage and black jazz pants.

"Hi," Kit said, holding out her hand. "I'm Kit Prestcott, the public relations manager at Hush. Welcome to the hotel."

"Hey, Kit," the woman said with a big smile. "Great to meet you." Her smile was charming, and her face was pretty, if a little too heavily made up for Kit's taste.

"I hope you have everything you need," Kit said politely.

A husky laugh greeted her. "I can't find Prince Charming under the bed. Other than that, I'm good. Come on in."

She turned and Kit decided the woman had exaggerated about her ass. It wasn't the size of Texas. More like Rhode Island.

"Based on your winning contest entry," Kit said, "your escort organized tickets to *Swan Lake* tonight. The ballet."

"No shit. I love ballet." Her face lit up, and then fell. "But I don't have anything to wear to a fancy schmancy ballet."

She flung open the double doors of the wardrobe and Kit had to agree.

Knowing nothing but disaster could result if this woman showed up as the elegant Giles's date in something too bright, too glittery and definitely too tight, she rashly decided that Piper would want this fantasy winner to have a new dress.

"I've got a surprise for you," she said. "Come on."

"What is it?"

"First, I'm going to take you on a hotel tour. I think you'll be impressed. Then we're going to visit the hotel boutique and get you a dress for tonight."

"Is that part of the prize? I don't remember reading anything about clothes."

"The prize is sort of based on you. It's all about having the most pampered, sensually stimulating weekend of your life."

She received a skeptically quirked eyebrow in reply.

"Come on," she said, "I'll show you."

They toured the hotel and soon Irene was giggling. They passed a middle-aged couple in a shadowed corner almost in flagrante delicto. As they took the elevator up, a room service waiter entered carrying a tray containing a bottle of champagne, a fresh tube of passion fruit personal lubricant and a cellophane-wrapped package of batteries.

"You know," Irene said, "Just looking at that stuff is making me horny."

Kit smiled. "There's a good stock of supplies in the bedside drawers in your room."

"Honey, battery-operated fun I can get at home. This weekend, I'm hoping for a cock that actually has a man attached to it."

Kit thought of Giles and this very frank woman together and felt the beginnings of a tension headache. "You know, your escort is strictly a host. There's no sex implied."

"Oh, sure. That was clear in the contest rules. That's okay. I figure if my escort isn't interested, there's got to be some guy around here who is. If I can't get laid in *this* hotel, then I might as well give up." She sighed as they got to the roof. The flowers had never looked so good since May Ellison had taken over their care. The pool winked invitingly, and a young man and woman snoozed on deck chairs, holding hands. "Although I might have forgotten how."

Kit looked over at the young couple. Newlyweds, she guessed, and thought about her own dry spell. "I know what you mean."

By the time they'd toured the library, the ballroom, and Exhibit A, Irene was back to giggling.

"Is there anywhere in this hotel you don't see people making out?"

"The lobby. Well, they do, of course, but we encourage them to visit our more private locations."

For the last stop on their tour, she took her contest winner, as promised, to the lobby boutique. Irene headed straight for a reed-slim green sheath that would look great on Iman but on Irene was going to look like a badly stuffed sausage gone to mould.

Kit shook her head, calling on her own tact and the woman's fantasy to guide her away from sartorial disaster. "That is not a princess dress."

She took her new friend by the hand and led her to a rack of gauzy, fantasy gowns. "This," she said, pulling out a pale pink Betsey Johnson with a fitted bodice and a bell skirt, "this is a princess dress."

Naturally, her first attempt at a fashion makeover wasn't an instant success. Irene snorted. "My fantasy is to be pampered like a princess, not look like Barbie does the Oscars."

But she didn't walk away. She reached past Kit and began flicking through the dresses. They were all fabulous. Part of the fantasy hung right there on the rack. Kit had never thought of herself as a fairy godmother, but there was something powerful about providing the clothes for a princess fantasy.

She watched, fascinated, as the cynical expression slowly melted from Irene's countenance. The eyes went first, from hard and bright to soft and dreamy. Then her mouth joined in, the I-laugh-at-life smirk smoothing into a wishful smile. Oh, that woman hadn't lied. She wanted to be a fairy princess for one weekend more than she wanted a sold-out crowd at The Comedy Club.

Kit watched Irene, not the rack, so she knew the second she'd discovered the dress that made her heart sing. Kit looked at the dress and though it wasn't pastel princess perfect, it wasn't remotely like anything else in Irene's wardrobe, either.

The dress was black, with a full skirt, made of tulle with a discreet scatter of rhinestones. "It's gorgeous."

When Irene glanced at the price tag, she sagged, but Kit, already used to the boutique's prices, and aware of the markup, patted her shoulder reassuringly. "Try it on."

A helpful young sales assistant found the dress in her size, found the perfect black, strappy shoes and even a swanky little clutch purse.

When Irene emerged from the change room, Kit thought she looked better than she'd imagined possible. It wasn't simply the dress, it was the still dreamy expression. She seemed softer, sweeter and more approachable.

"What do you think?" Irene asked, spinning so the black skirt belled around her, sparkling in the light.

"You look like Cinderella's sexy sister," she said.

"Her aunt, maybe. Her older, fatter, slutty aunt."

"Not in this dress," Kit promised. "Older, more sophisticated aunt."

"What did you have in mind for jewelry?" asked the sales clerk.

"I've got some big, chunky black beads."

The young woman, after a brief glance at Kit, shook her head and ran to the costume jewelry counter, returning with a slim chain with crystals and matching earrings. Kit was going to really have to explain her expense account after this. But then, knowing Piper, if she were here she'd be talking Irene into one of the faux fur stoles that cost more than an entire herd of skinned animals.

"We'll take all of it," said Kit. "Put it on my account, will you?"

"Sure, Kit."

"It's so expensive," Irene gasped, staring at her reflection as though she was having trouble believing it.

"It looks fabulous on you, and part of a fantasy is looking the part."

"Honey, you are so right."

While the sales clerk wrapped and packaged everything, Kit said, "So, what do you want to do before dinner?"

"I want an in-room massage," she said with so little hesitation Kit knew she'd already chosen it from the list of spa services.

"An excellent choice." She glanced up. "May I recommend we add a manicure, pedicure and makeup and hair styling to that?"

Irene's laugh was the sort that made you want to join in. Probably a real asset in her profession. "I like the way you think."

"I'll send somebody up. What do you want to do about dinner? Before the ballet in Amuse Bouche, our amazing restaurant? Or after the show?"

"After, I think. I might take a nap after my massage."

"All right. There are four of us going to the ballet. I'll send your escort to pick you up at your room at six, if that's okay. We thought we'd have drinks in Erotique and then head to the ballet in the Hush limo."

"Great."

"If you want a snack to tide you over until after the ballet, our room service menu is quite extensive."

"Are you kidding? I'm on a diet from this second until I sit down at the restaurant. If you have an anticellulite massage, book me that."

Good. If Irene was busy all afternoon, then Kit had some time to run down to the spa and check on Peter. She also needed to organize dinner on the roof. The thought of her and Peter alone on the roof having a midnight supper sent a quick chill up her spine.

"What's he like?" Irene's voice interrupted a vision of her and Peter on the roof, and they were not eating dinner.

Kit turned to Irene. "Peter?"

"Is that his name? My Prince Charming?"

"Right. Sorry. I was thinking of something else. Your escort is named Giles. He's British."

"Sweet. Is he cute?"

"I'd say he's more…" she thought of the lean face and the upright bearing. "More aristocratic-looking than cute."

"Aristocratic? Wow. You took this whole Prince Charming thing pretty seriously, huh."

"We really want to make this weekend memorable for you, Irene."

"Yeah, so what is he really, this Giles? An out-of-work actor?"

She'd come so close to guessing the identity of the original escort that Kit breathed a sigh of relief to be able to deny that Giles was an actor. "He's a businessman. I'll let him tell you about himself when you meet him tonight."

9

Second Fantasy Weekend winner: Irene Bonnet is
in Oscar suite. Winner is a professional comedienne. Give her anything she wants except material for her next gig. Be professional at all times.

Kit felt honor-bound, as his escort for the weekend,
to check on Peter in the spa. Since not even Piper herself could waltz in on a client during a facial, Kit was
deprived of the vision of Peter with his head wrapped
in a towel, some kind of colored paste all over his face
and cucumber rounds on his eyes.

But she could certainly use her imagination and picture him thus. Revenge was foolish, and she didn't believe in something so negative and so centered on events
from the past. She was human, though, so she pictured
a pink mask—maybe strawberry, as Piper had suggested.

However, when she got to the spa, she got her reward.
Peter and Giles were all done with their facials and
were side by side having their pedicures.

"Hi, boys," she said.

Peter's face told the whole story when he looked up
at her. He was mortified at having such a girlie proce-

dure, but she was pretty sure there was a part of him that was loving the pampering.

"Isn't the foot massage the best?" she asked brightly.

"You know, I've discovered there's a spa room for two here," he said, "I planned to be in it this afternoon. With you."

Since he was so adorably annoyed and he looked so cute with his feet in the paraffin wax, she leaned forward and kissed him.

"Your skin looks radiant," she whispered in his ear. "Really, you look years younger."

"I'm going to get you for this," he whispered back. "You know that, don't you."

She sent him a brief and, she hoped, enigmatic smile.

"I'll look forward to it."

"How's my princess?" Giles asked, seeming much more comfortable in the spa environment than poor Peter.

How to answer that? "She's…well, she's very nice. Good sense of humor."

"Sounds like a troll," Peter said.

"I wouldn't have put it so crudely, dear boy. But that's pretty much what I was thinking."

"Of course she isn't a troll. She's a very nice woman and I want you both to behave tonight. Please. My job depends on it."

To her enormous surprise, Giles took her hand and kissed it. "You may depend on me."

How did he do that? How did a man wearing nothing but a terry cloth robe and with his feet in plastic bags of wax manage to sound like a knight on a white charger?

"You aren't really a prince, are you?" she asked.

He laughed softly. "Lord, no. I've played polo once

or twice against HRH. That's as close to royalty as I'm likely to come." He glanced from one to the other of their astonished faces. "Younger son, you see."

"Pardon?" asked Kit, who didn't see at all.

"My elder brother inherited the title."

"Title?" Peter asked, looking for a moment as though the rest of him were going to turn to paraffin wax.

"My father was an earl. It's a hereditary title, of course."

"So you just missed a title?"

"By about four years. I'm afraid I'm just an *Honorable*. The family still hangs on to the estate, but that belongs to my brother now. I'm a commoner."

"You're an Honorable. You've never told me that before."

"It never came up. Besides, only intolerable snobs go about boasting of titles and so on. I hope I've got more sense."

"You are so perfect," Kit said, beaming and leaning forward to give Giles a kiss on the cheek.

"No, really," he said, looking bashful. "Happy to oblige."

"Are you coming in for a treatment?" Peter asked, glancing hopefully toward the spa room for two.

"I don't have time. I've got a few details to see to and then I have to dress for the ballet. Oh, and Giles, your date Irene has requested dinner after the ballet. I've booked one of the best tables in Amuse Bouche."

"Excellent. I'll enjoy trying the restaurant."

"See you later, then."

"I'll collect my date and we'll meet you in the bar, then. About six?"

"Wonderful." She waved goodbye to the two men and left.

PETER WATCHED KIT leave and thought he might have run after her had his feet not been currently sealed in bags of wax that squished between his toes and felt as ridiculous as he no doubt appeared.

Giles was looking at him with tolerant amusement, clearly much more at ease in this shrine to all things girlie than he could ever be. Okay, so they weren't the only men in the place, but it was a pretty small percentage of men to women. Take out the gay guys and he figured the number was maybe one.

Him.

The pedicurist removed the first bag of wax from his foot and just as she was easing his toes out, they heard a scream.

Peter jerked in his pink leather pedicure chair. The pedicurist didn't even glance up. "What was that?" he asked.

"A Brazilian," the woman said.

"Excitable people, South Americans," he said to Giles.

His old friend chuckled softly. "I think she means the woman who screeched is getting a Brazilian bikini wax."

Peter blanched. He'd heard of them; okay, he'd seen his fair share and he was quite a fan, but he really, really didn't want to think of one being performed quite so near him.

"That's right," the woman now applying some sort of goopy cream to his feet said. "We do a lot of waxing." She glanced up and gave them both a professional smile. "For men, too."

"What?" Peter instinctively put a hand over his privates. He thought he might have made a run for it if his feet weren't so slippery he'd be flat on his ass on that marble floor in a second. Or on his back with a couple of herniated disks. "Men get that?"

A chorus of chuckles met his horrified exclamation. "No. Not the Brazilian. Mostly for men we wax the back."

Giles's pedicurist nodded. "And the shoulders."

"Sometimes the butt."

"Got it," he said, a little louder than he meant to. "Thanks."

"I'm looking forward to this evening," Giles said, in an obvious ploy to change the subject.

Peter was only too happy to help him do it. "Are you? You sure helped Kit out of a jam. And me. She would have spent all day trying to nail some guy down if it weren't for you."

"She takes her job seriously. I like that about her."

"Yeah. She does."

"She's beautiful, too. Difficult not to like that in a woman."

"You really think she's beautiful?"

"Gorgeous. Don't you?"

"Yes," he said. "I do."

"How's the campaign going?"

"Campaign?"

Giles mouthed, so the busy pedicurists wouldn't hear him, "To win her back."

How was it going? Well, they'd had spectacular sex. That was good. She had left right after. Not so good. He'd thought his plan for the day had been a stroke of brilliance, but she'd seen right through his ploy and ended up making a fool of him, sticking him in the pedicure zone with Giles when he wanted to be in the Treatments for Two room with her.

"Hard to say," he said at last. "I've made some progress but there's still a way to go."

"Mmm. And not a great deal of time."

Peter blinked. He hadn't thought of his plan to win back Kit in those terms, but Giles was right. After this weekend, she was under no obligation to see him again. He had less than twenty-four hours to get her—if not back, then at least willing to keep seeing him.

What the hell was he doing having his toenails buffed?

Disengaging his feet from the woman working on them, he said, "I'm sorry. I don't have time for this."

"But I'm almost done. I only buffed one foot."

"Really, Peter. You'll look barely civilized."

"I'll have to trust you to keep my secrets," he said, and sped away to change.

Kit's cell phone rang.

"Hi, Kit. It's Janice."

Her heart sank. What more could possibly go wrong? "What's up?" she asked, her smile as firm and her tone as upbeat as ever.

"Your contest winner is looking for you."

"Which one?"

"Peter."

"But he's in the spa."

"Not anymore. He asked you to drop by his suite. He said it's urgent."

She let out a huff of exasperation. "Any idea what the emergency is?"

"No."

"I really don't have time—"

"Anything he wants. That's your rule with these guys, remember?"

Janice was right, which only annoyed her all the more. Peter was a manipulative weasel, but there was nothing she could do about it. Until noon tomorrow.

Checkout had never sounded so good.

"I'll be right there. Thanks Janice."

"No problem. Um, you did say anything he wants, right?"

"Within reason, my budget and the law, yes."

"Okay. Just checking."

What on earth?

Kit left her office, giving Eartha Kitty a final snuggle. The cat, who was pouting around the offices in Piper's absence, had greeted her as if she were an entire tub of catnip, so Kit hadn't accomplished much. In truth, she was basically hiding out, anyway.

But not anymore.

"Sorry, baby. I have to go babysit an overgrown spoiled brat."

She took the time to brush her hair and teeth and freshen her lip gloss before making her way to Peter's suite. She wasn't primping for him, she told herself. She always tried to look her best in front of the guests.

Once more, she found herself knocking on the door to Peter's suite. The last time she'd done this, she'd been wearing the black dress and the sexy black underwear. She shivered slightly as images of last night played around her mind the way Eartha Kitty had circled her ankles earlier.

Think about something else.

She tried, and an image of Peter in the chair getting a pedicure took hold. Good, this was good. Peter in a Hush robe.

Naked under the robe.

Shut up!

Try again. But before she could think of anything that didn't somehow involve Peter being naked, he was opening the door.

He was still in his robe and a pair of spa slippers, which meant that underneath the robe he was still...

Naked.

"Oh," she said, as images and desires and memories crowded her. "I can wait until you're dressed."

"No," he said. "Come in."

She did, walking in gingerly.

"Oh," she said again.

The big, gorgeous bath was bubbling away, and there was the heavenly smell of scented candles in the air. It wasn't dark outside, but Peter had turned off all the lights in the suite and lit the candles anyway, so they glowed as though the tub sported a halo.

Fresh ice was in the ice bucket, and the champagne was as ready to pop as she was.

"I thought we'd get ready for the ballet together," he said.

"But my things are all—"

"They're all in here."

"What?"

"Janice, the general manager, took care of it for me."

"Janice? But—" She stopped. Of course, that must be what Janice had meant about giving in to all Peter's requests. Okay, so technically, having her clothes and makeup and things moved to his suite was within in her budget and it wasn't illegal. But was it reasonable?

She glanced at Peter who was watching her as though he knew exactly what was going through her head.

"Remember," he said softly, "anything I want."

She could grab her things and walk out that door right now, and they both knew it.

Or she could sink into that bath—one of her greatest weaknesses, as Peter well knew.

"Come on, it will do you good. Get some of the tension out of your shoulders. I'll even massage them for you, since you missed your spa appointment today."

She looked at him with her brows raised. "You brought me here to massage my shoulders?"

The grin didn't quite make it to his mouth, but it sure as hell was putting devil lights in his eyes. "Among other things."

Then he moved closer. "Come on. I was a good sport about spending my spa date with Giles. How about you giving me a break?"

It was pretty tough to argue when the bubbling tub called to her insistently, and a tiny crack came from the direction of the ice bucket, as though the champagne was begging to be opened, and oh, yeah, under his robe Peter was...

He kissed her and then grinned.

"What?"

"You brushed your teeth."

"I—"

"Hope you were thinking of kissing me when you were freshening up. I was so anxious to get you alone I only got one foot buffed."

She marched over to the hook on the wall and took down one of the luxury robes, then headed for the bathroom.

"Hey," Peter said, "where are you going?"

"I'm getting changed."

"You can do that out here."

"I don't think so." She sent him a wicked smile. "Striptease was last night."

It was crazy and dangerous to play these kind of games with Peter, her inner voice tried to tell her as she stripped off her clothes in the bathroom.

But she was in no danger. Maybe a couple of years ago, spending a no-strings, sexy weekend with him would have been impossible, but she'd grown up a lot. She was tougher, smarter and very much her own woman. She played games now that she hadn't even heard about back in her college days.

Hell, you didn't survive the Manhattan singles life if you weren't a tough, smart, independent games player.

Her toiletry bag was sitting on the counter, and no doubt her dress and accessories were neatly hanging in one of the closets. She scooped her hair out of the collar of the robe, dug out a hair clip from her bag and fastened her hair in a sloppy bun, then belted the robe around her naked and frankly eager body and headed back into the main room.

Her date was just easing the cork out of the champagne with a quiet *pop*. He poured wine into two flutes with the Hush logo stamped on them and waited for her to reach him.

She held out a hand but he shook his head, his gaze holding hers. "I'll pass it to you when you're in the bath," he said.

"Fine," she agreed, and unbelted the robe, then shrugged it from her shoulders so it tumbled to the floor.

"I never get tired of looking at you," he said, his gaze traveling slowly down her naked body. "You're more beautiful than ever."

She stepped into the bath slowly, aware that her nipples were puckering under his ardent gaze. Ignoring him as best she could, she let the water swirl around her lower legs, mildly annoyed that the temperature of the water was exactly the way she liked it. She sank down into the water. The tubs were amazing. It was like sitting in a lounger, but with bubbling water soothing her tense muscles and a view of Manhattan out the window. The candles flickered softly as Peter passed her champagne.

He shucked his own robe and she noted that his body was just as gorgeous as it had been last night. Even as she gazed at him, arousal took hold of them both. She felt desire in her own body, watched it rise in his.

"Tough to be a man," he said when her lips quirked. "All your thoughts show."

He seemed more cheerful than embarrassed and certainly didn't hurry to bury himself under bubbles. He took his sweet time sitting at the other end of this tub for two. Piper had spent what was probably an insignificant amount for Piper but had seemed like a lot to Kit on doing something or other so the tubs were almost silent. "I can't stand being in a tub that sounds like you're in a steam train roaring through a tunnel, you know?" Piper had said. At the time, Kit had thought it was another rich girl princess thing, but now that she was in the tub, the near silence was fantastic.

When Peter was settled back, bubbles burbling around his shoulders, he gazed over at her and raised his glass.

"To old friends," Kit said, before he could speak.

"To old friends," he echoed solemnly. "And new love."

She'd taken a sip of the crisp champagne after she'd spoken, so his addendum to the toast caught her by surprise, making her swallow the wrong way so that she spluttered and choked.

"Who said anything about love?" she gasped, blinking. Her voice sounded hoarse.

"What's wrong with love?"

Was he insane? "Nothing. I'm all for it. Just not with you."

"But we made love, last night."

"There are a lot of terms in common usage to describe what we did last night."

"One of them, and I'm willing to bet it's the one you most commonly use, is making love." His freshly pedicured toes trailed up her leg to her knee. She pretended not to notice.

"What's your point?"

"I'm saying there's a lot of history between us, and maybe some love."

She narrowed her gaze. "You said 'new love.'"

He gazed at her earnestly. "I'm feeling a lot of things since I found you again. I love…" She glared at him so hard he ought to be tossed out, wet and sudsy, onto the carpet… "I love who you've become."

"I love the way they do yellowfin tuna at Nobu."

"You didn't used to be this tough."

"No," she said, sipping more champagne. "I didn't. Is that part of the new me you love?"

"Sometimes."

He put his glass down on the handy indentation on the side of the tub and scooted forward. "I also love the way you wear your hair now, and the color."

"I was always blond, Peter."

"I mean those highlights or streaks or whatever you call the lighter parts."

Damn, he was more observant than she'd thought.

"Looks great. Very sophisticated." Then he pulled

the clip from her hair and as her hair tumbled down he pushed his hands through the strands. Then he kissed her.

His lips were cool and tasted of champagne, but only for a second until their mouths warmed each other. His hands trailed down her body, already sensitized by the bubbling warm water, so she felt stimulated everywhere.

Usually, she hated sex in a tub. There wasn't enough room, water sloshed everywhere, the taps and faucet got in the way. Kit had decided aquatic sex was totally overrated.

But, of course, this tub, being a Hush installation, was somehow different. The taps and faucet were out of the way on the side, the tub was deep enough that water didn't slosh anywhere it shouldn't and since it was built for two (at least) there was plenty of room.

And then there were the jets that gently massaged every part of her body. Mmm. And his hands became somehow part of the tub's delights, massaging and kneading, providing a different, firmer rhythm than the soft jets of water.

The condom was slightly awkward, and she was tempted to tell him she was on the Pill. She was clean and careful, and unless he'd changed more than she'd believe possible, he was, too. But did she want that kind of intimacy? Without so much as a sheath of latex between them?

No, she decided. She did not. So she let him fumble the thing onto his wet flesh. Then she leaned over, kissed him hard, and rode him.

Splish, splash.

Sure, she no longer thought about Peter and forever in the same sentence, but he was still the best sex she'd ever had.

10

IRENE HAD NEVER FELT more stupid in her life as she stood staring at herself in the mirror. The Hush team had spent a couple of hours on hair, makeup, stuffing her into this dress and heels that gave her blisters just opening the shoe box.

She looked like Sharon Osborne on a bad day. And before the face lifts. Who was she kidding? She wasn't the princess type.

She was thirty-seven years old. A Midwestern car mechanic's daughter. A woman who'd learned young that if you kept cracking jokes, you had control of a room. Not only that, but if nobody knew the tough gal with the tough mouth yearned for romance, then nobody could hurt her.

Now she'd let the secret out and all she wanted to do was stuff it deep inside again where it wouldn't expose her to hurt.

This was ridiculous. That wasn't her staring back in the mirror with those big, wide eyes and the soft pink mouth. Pink? When had she ever worn pink on her lips. Oh, no. She was red all the way, baby. Scarlet, in fact.

Pulling open the wardrobe, she dragged out something red and black. Hard to see because her vision had gone wavery. Oh, great. Stick her in a poufed dress and she started sniveling. Nope. Not her.

Okay, so they'd spent a fortune on her appearance, but this weekend was about having anything she wanted, and if she wanted to change her mind and be an almost middle-aged woman instead of a princess, then that's exactly what she'd do.

On her hands and knees, she dug out the bright red Keds she bought in bulk at Target and dragged off one of the tippy, strappy things that were probably Manolo Blahnik. She snorted. Like anybody had ever heard of him before *Sex and the City.* Now women like her, who lived in the Midwest and never got nearer Manhattan than sitting in front of their televisions on Friday night, knew which shoe designers were cool. Shoe designers, for cripes sake!

Maybe that's why she liked her red Keds. She could pronounce the name of the shoe and, big bonus, not cripple herself while wearing them or, even worse, fall flat on her face.

She had one red Ked and one black Blahnik going on when there was a soft knock on the door.

People had been parading in and out all afternoon to do things to her. Hair, eyebrow wax, which she hadn't asked for and could only assume the hairdresser had ordered. Or Kit. Facial, manicure, pedicure, makeup. Now what? Were they planning to rub the deodorant on her underarms?

She opened the door and then nearly fell over, for which the uneven stance of trying to balance in one flat shoe and one stiletto was doubtless to blame. It couldn't have been the dreamboat standing there.

For a second she simply stared up into the epitome of every prince she'd ever imagined. He was tall, naturally; dark, of course, though there were just a scattering of silver threads to make him look distinguished. His eyes were gray and cool and superior, but with a hint of a smile. His brows rose slightly when she stood there tottering, ridiculously off balance, and staring.

"Irene Bonnet?" he inquired in such perfect, toffee-nosed, pompous, upper-class Britspeak that she nearly swooned. Oh, man. Swooned. Now she was even think-ing like a dim-witted princess overcome by some hand-some dude who'd give her thirteen children before she was twenty-five and be forever riding off to fight drag-ons or crusades or modern architecture in London, or whatever princes did.

"Yeah. Yes. I'm Irene. And you are?"

"I'm your escort for this evening. Giles Pendleton."

Then the dreamboat presented her with a corsage. An honest-to-God corsage with a perfect, white flower. She felt weak and swoony. *Snap out of it,* she snarled to herself.

"Where did they get you? Central casting?" she found herself saying.

"Kent, actually. My family home is in Kent."

"Well, it sure as hell isn't in Ohio." He couldn't be for real, but then this whole weekend was about fantasy, so who really cared. For all she knew, he was from Ohio and he'd learned that accent in acting school. Yep, he could have grown up down the road from where she was raised. Stuffed into a tux, with his hair perfect and that bred-to-be-snooty expression he was channeling, he looked fabulous.

"Sit down," he said, "and let me help you with your other shoe."

Because she was still momentarily stunned that they'd whipped up this guy as though they'd crawled in-

side her head and taken the specs, she did sit down—
plonk—in one of the armchairs.

Before her stunned eyes, PC knelt gracefully on one
knee and slipped the sneaker off her foot, replacing it
with the black stiletto before she'd pulled together
enough of her wits to let him know she planned to wear
sneakers.

"Thanks," she said, letting him help her to her feet.

"May I pin your corsage?"

She nodded. He was so deft, his fingers barely touched
her and yet there was a warm sliding of his fingers against
her shoulder as he pinned the flowers to her dress.

"How did you know?" she asked. "How did you
know I wasn't wearing white?"

"I'd like to pretend it was my inate exquisite taste,
but in fact I cheated and phoned Kit. She knew what you
were wearing."

Yeah, because she'd picked it out and paid for it. Obviously, she hadn't said so to his lordship, here, for
which she was absurdly grateful.

She picked up her clutch, cast a last, hopeless glance
at her comfortable black and red clothes and the flat
shoes, then took a nervous breath,

"You look beautiful," Giles said in that soft but
sexy voice.

She looked once again at herself in the mirror. "You
don't think I look like one of those dusters made with
ostrich feathers?"

He chuckled. "No. I think you look like the sort of
woman who has season's tickets to the ballet."

"Charm school as well as acting lessons, huh?" She
smiled at him, feeling more relaxed now that she knew
she at least had a dreamboat for a date.

His eyes crinkled attractively at the corners. He held out his arm, crooked. "Shall we?" he asked, then took her hand and placed it on his arm.

"So," she said, "would I have seen you in anything?"

He gazed down at her in a puzzled fashion. "I'm not sure I know what you mean."

"Like movies or plays?" She didn't want him to think she expected too much, so she added, "Commercials? Department store flyers?" Maybe that's why he seemed familiar. She could imagine him modeling for Burberry or bowler hats.

He seemed quite amused. "I'm not an actor."

"Huh? What are you then? I mean, when you're not in the escort business."

"I'm a businessman."

"Well, that's elucidating and pretty much covers everything from drug running to file clerking."

"I do neither, though I'm afraid the excitement and danger of my work are closer to file clerking than drug smuggling."

"Do I keep guessing or are you going to tell me?"

"I'm in banking, actually. Private banking."

"Cool. In England?"

"Primarily, yes. Although we've got a number of clients in America so we'll be opening up a branch here in New York in a few months."

She was stunned. Could her prince be gainfully employed? Of course, the whole snooty private banking résumé could have been invented for her benefit. It didn't really matter, since he only had to fake it for a weekend. But she'd like to know. A simple experiment should prove whether he was banking on her ignorance of banking to get through the evening.

"So," she said, casually, "where do you think the Dow's headed in the next couple of months. Is it still a better bet than NASDAQ?"

Giles patted the hand tucked into his arm. "One should never mix business and pleasure, my dear," he said, which was totally cute and absolutely in character, and managed to skirt around the fact that he probably knew less about what she was talking about than she did. The only stocks in her portfolio were the hundred shares of Apple she had bought after she had fallen in love with her pink iPod and decided that a company that could make any product that adorable deserved her money.

They reached the bar too soon for Irene, who was enjoying walking arm in arm with the sexiest Brit on earth. Erotique, for heaven's sake. Somebody had been drinking too many Bellinis when they named this place.

Giles glanced around and said, "It looks as though we're the first. Shall we go in?"

"Sure."

He led them to a table not far from the bar and with a good view of the entrance. He waited until Irene was seated before sitting down himself. What manners!

"What will you have to drink?"

"I don't know. I usually have rum and Coke, but I feel like I should drink something elegant with this dress on."

"Most definitely. May I suggest a champagne cocktail?"

"Is it as good as it sounds?"

"Yes."

She grinned at him. "Okay. I'm game."

Giles made the smallest motion with his hand and suddenly a waiter appeared. He was obviously the sort of man who got good tables in restaurants and could always get a cab in New York.

"Yes, sir. What can I get for you and the lady?"

"A champagne cocktail for my companion, please, and I'll have a dry martini."

"Straight up?"

"Naturally."

After the waiter left, Giles said, "What is so amusing?"

"You are." She mimicked the waiter, "Straight up?" and then really piled on the British accent, "Naturally." She was a gifted mimic, and Giles was forced to smile even if he didn't find it all that delightful that she was making fun of him. Always one to blather on when anyone else would shut up, she added, "How do you like your sex, sir? Straight up?" and then answered herself, "Naturally."

He looked more startled than annoyed. "Did Peter tell you that?"

"Peter who?"

"Ah, never mind. I've a notion that Peter thinks—"

But whatever it was that Peter thought she obviously wasn't going to find out. Giles rose gracefully, as Kit arrived dragging a total hottie along with her. They both seemed a little breathless and had that "just sexed" look about them that made Irene envious. The hottie's hair was damp.

"Sorry we're late," Kit said.

"Not at all," Giles replied. "We only just arrived ourselves. What will you have to drink? Irene's going to try a champagne cocktail."

"That sounds good to me," Kit said.

"And I'm having a martini." He glanced at the cutie, who nodded, then walked over to the bar.

Her attention was caught by Kit who said, "Irene, this is Peter."

"Hi," she said, and they shook hands.

The fresh-out-of-bed twosome seemed as if they were having trouble coming down to earth, so Irene said, "This is a great bar."

"Yes." Peter glanced at Kit under his ridiculously-long-for-a-man eyelashes and said, "And this is my favorite table."

Kit blinked, and glanced around. She did the strangest thing; she leaned down to look underneath. "Is this the one?"

"Yep."

"The one what?"

"This is the table where Kit and I sat last time we had a drink in this bar. A brandy," he said, with another wicked glance at Kit. No wonder the poor woman was blushing. If Giles started looking at her with that unadorned lust, she'd be blushing, too. Although the very idea of Giles acting so…American seemed as unlikely as any man looking at her as though he couldn't wait to drag her off to bed.

Not that she wasn't a sexy woman; she was. But few men bothered to make love to her with their hot gazes. Unfortunately.

Giles returned to his seat beside hers and behind him came their waiter with four drinks.

He'd been right, she found when she tasted her cocktail. She did like it. Very much. It was elegant. Not too sweet and not too dry.

"How's the champagne cocktail?"

"Just right."

There was silence for a moment and then Peter said to Giles, "I bumped into Duncan Trevor coming out of the restaurant."

"Good lord. I wonder what he's doing here?"

"I don't know. But I hope whatever he's doing, he's doing it with his wife. I heard they were getting back together."

"Oh, good. He's a nice chap."

"Didn't you arrange the financing for his company?"

"Yes."

Irene blinked. Financing for a company? Could he really be in banking? Or was Peter part of the show? Determined to get the truth, she said, "Giles."

"Yes?"

She held out her perfectly manicured hand, the nails painted a pale pink that exactly matched her lipstick. "Hand me your business card."

He dug out his wallet with no hesitation and drew out a card that was so discreet he could have been a secret agent. The stock was a rich cream and the inscription said The Honorable Giles Pendleton, Private Banking. There were some letters after his name, and the address of the bank was London. England.

"Is this for real?"

"I'm afraid so," he said, as though he were apologizing.

Not entirely sure she believed him, she glanced at the other two. "He's really in banking?"

They both nodded.

"He's not an actor?"

They both shook their heads.

"What's all this about The Honorable?" she wanted to know.

"It's on your business card?" Peter said, looking stunned.

"I carry two business cards, to be honest," Giles said.

"You're really a secret agent, aren't you?"

He chuckled softly. "Well, I like that better than an actor, at any rate."

She tucked the business card into her new clutch that contained breath mints, twenty bucks in case she needed cab fare home, a lipstick and a comb.

Kit, who was born to be in public relations, eased them into a new subject so fast it could have been greased. "I bet your job is really interesting, being a stand-up comic."

"Well, it beats keypunch operator, and when I started out, those were my options."

Kit laughed. "Where do you get your material?"

Funny how everyone asked that question first. She shrugged. "It comes from life, I guess. From looking at something a new way. Like…my feet are killing me in these shoes. I'd like to make fun of Manolo Blahnik right now."

"Really?" Kit's eyes shone. "Why don't you?"

"What, now?"

"Sure."

The men nodded. She didn't usually give impromptu performances, but she'd never been a shy person, so she said, "Okay. This is totally raw and if it flops, I don't want to hear about it. Let's see. You know, I really got into the business because of Bob Newhart. I love his old routines. So, this is a phone routine."

She took a breath, steadied herself. "I'm a clerk at Vital Statistics, I'm on the phone and I'm trying to register Manolo Blahnik's birth."

She glanced around and they all nodded.

"Blanket?" she whined in a Brooklyn accent. "His name's Blanket? Isn't that kind of a crappy name for a baby?"

Some nodding, and mmm-hmming on her pretend telephone.

"Oh, well, well, if it's his last name, I guess he's stuck with it. What does it rhyme with?"

Long pause. She loved watching a live audience, even such a small one. She could see their little mental wheels whirring collectively trying to come up with rhymes for Blahnik.

After a good, long pause, she shook her head and said into the telephone, "Does it rhyme with anything in English?"

"Maybe you should spell it."

"Aha. All right," her ersatz clerk finally said, wiping her brow with relief. "And what's the first name?"

She rolled the word *Manolo* around on her tongue, even as she rolled her eyes to the three people watching her.

"Honey, with a name like that, he'd better be an astronaut." Long pause. "Or a shoe designer."

They all laughed, but she thought they were genuinely amused. "That was great," Kit said. "Did you really just make it up?"

"Sure. If I worked on it I'd make it funnier."

"You should, then," Giles said.

"You're right. I could do a series of short pieces on designers." She tapped her nails on the bar, thinking. "Anybody got a pen? I have to write this down before I forget."

Giles passed her a pen that had such a nice heft and

feel that it had to be expensive. With the aid of his pen and three more of his fancy business cards, she managed to scrawl down the basis of her new idea.

"Thanks," she said, when she raised her head. She returned Giles's pen and popped the four scribbled-on business cards in her purse.

"Wow, that was so much fun," Kit said, then suddenly frowned. "Um, you're not going to make fun of our contest are you?"

Startled, she glanced straight at Giles. Why, she didn't know. He smiled at her reassuringly, giving her confidence that he, at least, didn't see this whole thing as a joke.

"No," Irene said. "Of course not."

They whiled away the rest of the drinks time discussing ballets they had seen. The tally was: Giles had seen pretty much everything performed in London or New York in the last two and a half decades; Irene had seen everything featured on PBS and danced by The Ohio Ballet; Kit's tally was four ballets since she'd moved to Manhattan. Peter, zero.

"Aren't you a fantasy winner, too?" she asked Peter.

He glanced at Kit as though he wanted to pop her in his mouth like the olive in his drink. "Oh, yeah."

"Then what are you doing coming along to this ballet if it's not your thing?"

He was still gazing at Kit, who was pretending not to notice. "I wanted to try something new. And, for the record, I'm having a perfect fantasy weekend," he said.

Kit glanced at him quickly and Irene thought there was something very complicated going on between them. Observing people was her hobby as well as an occupational necessity, and she was fairly certain there was more than a fantasy weekend going on between those two.

Interesting.

"Well," Giles said, "I'm glad that's settled. Shall we go?"

She rose first. "Yes, Your Lordship," she said, and curtseyed.

"Actually," he said, "it's my elder brother you would address as Your Lordship. I'm a younger son."

And she, who in her whole life had never been stumped for something to say, was struck dumb.

He really was a kind of royalty. There had to be something major wrong with this guy and she was determined to figure out what before she got carried away with this fantasy thing.

Her silence continued through the first act of the ballet. She barely breathed, she was so entranced. She was glad they weren't seeing something modern. She wanted a fairy tale, she wanted white, delicate tutus. She wanted *Swan Lake*.

She barely spoke during the intermission, and when they got to the dying swan scene, the tears ran unchecked down her face since the four items in her clutch did not include tissues. How stupid of her.

She tried to wipe her cheeks with her hand without ruining her makeup job and suddenly Giles reached into a pocket and handed her a big, white, linen handkerchief.

She didn't even take her eyes off the stage, simply mopped her face and then reached out with her hand and found his.

Wordlessly, he clasped her hand in a comforting hold. She felt warmth and a strange kind of kinship between them. Odd, because they couldn't be more different, and yet there was something about Giles that she recognized. He was an outsider too, she thought, and as much of an observer of life as she was. She might crack jokes, while he merely watched his world with lazy amusement, but there was still a natural sympathy between them.

"Oh, that was so wonderful. Thank you," she said when the final bows had been taken and she'd clapped so hard and so long she was verging on carpal tunnel syndrome.

"You're welcome," Giles said, looking down at her with a glinting smile.

"Oh, God, you're staring. Is my makeup a total mess?"

"It's fine. I'm so glad you enjoyed the ballet."

"Enjoyed? I loved it so much. If I lived here, I'd go to every performance, I think." She tried to hand him back his very damp handkerchief but he shook his head.

"Keep it."

"But it's monogrammed. The serfs must have worked night and day sewing your initials onto it."

"There haven't been any serfs under my family for four hundred years," he said in that snooty way that charmed her silly. "And my handkerchiefs are made in France. You can blow your nose on this one with a clear conscience."

"Okay." She smiled mistily up at him and did exactly that.

She would have sat there all night, probably, staring at the curtain, replaying the ballet. The aisles were crowded as the other patrons made their way out of the theatre, conversation buzzed and cell phones appeared to be surreptitiously turned back on, but she was still lost.

"Well, that was fabulous," said Kit.

"Wasn't it?" She turned to Peter. "Did you like it?"

"It wasn't nearly as bad as I thought it would be," he admitted.

"You, Peter, are a philistine."

Peter opened his mouth, but Kit laughed softly and put her hand on her date's shoulder. "Don't be too hard on him, Giles. He was a good sport." She kissed him softly. "Thanks. I really enjoyed it." She turned to the two of them. "The limo will pick us up. You're eating at Amuse Bouche, right?"

"Yes," said Irene. "I read this fantastic review in the in-flight magazine." She glanced at Giles. "If that's okay with you."

"Tonight, I am at your command."

And when he said them, those campy words didn't even sound corny. She sighed.

"Are you in a hurry to get back?" he asked, still looking at her with that faint smile that made her feel more like a princess than this fabulous dress ever could.

"No." She was in the middle of a fairy tale and in no hurry to get out of it.

He turned back to Kit. "I think perhaps we'll find our own way back."

"Okay," Kit said. "I'll tell the restaurant you'll be late."

"Thanks." Giles gave her his charming smile, and Peter and Kit joined the crowd exiting the theatre. They fit well together, Irene thought.

Then she and Giles left their seats and joined the mass of ballet lovers wearing everything from diamonds and furs to jeans and ball caps.

"Would you like to go backstage and meet the dancers?" he asked softly.

"You could make that happen?"

"Yes."

She thought about it. Did she want to see those magical creatures up close and personal? Did she want to see the twisted feet and sweat-streaked makeup and reality? "No," she breathed. "I don't. I want to remember it as it was."

"Come on, then. It's a beautiful evening in one of the greatest cities in the world. We'll walk."

"In these shoes?" She raised her foot so he could see the ice-pick heels that were at least seventeen inches high.

"Ah."

He didn't say any more but she could tell he had a plan so she hobbled along behind him. The next thing she knew, she was being handed up into a horse-drawn carriage.

Hey, wait a minute, the snarky smart-ass part of her said. *This is like a total cliché. God, what if somebody sees me?*

Then the horse clopped on its way, she tilted her head back to stare at the trees, the sky and the buildings, and she thought, what the hell.

"What are you smiling about?" Giles asked from closer than she'd realized.

She turned her head and there he was, inches away. "I was thinking what a cliché I am. A middle-aged tourist on a two-bit pony ride in New York. All I need is a collection of I heart the Big Apple shot glasses and I'm all set."

Giles chuckled. "I adore your honesty."

"You do?"

"Yes. I think I got as much pleasure watching you enjoy the ballet as I received from the ballet itself."

"You were watching me?" She'd been so enthralled she hadn't even noticed.

"You were enchanting."

"What time is it?" she asked her escort.

Looking vaguely surprised, he glanced at the slim and elegant gold watch on his wrist. "It's almost ten past eleven."

"Tell the driver to spring the horse so it can get me home before it turns into a rat, or a pumpkin, or I turn into a pumpkin. I don't know, it's been a long time since I read Cinderella. But there are pumpkins involved."

Giles took her hand. "Why are you so certain this evening can't be real?"

"Oh, the evening's real enough, I guess. It's you who can't possibly be for real."

He didn't look offended, more puzzled. "Why not?"

"Because you are a contest prize. Believing in you would be like thinking the plastic ring in my Cracker Jack box was a real diamond."

"Do I truly have to prove to you that I am Giles Pendleton?"

"The Honorable Giles Pendleton, whose brother is a lord."

"But I am those things. I'm also a man."

She'd never shied from honestly and she didn't now. "Yeah, well, you may be all those things, but guys with Honorable on their business cards who talk like they're taking tea with Queen Elizabeth don't usually go out with me."

"I see. So it's not me you don't believe in, Irene." Giles said, gazing at her. "It's yourself."

For a second, she stared back at him, seeing something like understanding, maybe even recognition. She took refuge, as she always did when her emotions scared her, in wisecracking.

"Really, you should see my usual dates. Don't get me started. The last time a guy went down on me, we were Rollerblading and I tripped him. I was—"

Giles interrupted her poor-me-I'm-a-dating-disaster monologue by leaning over and kissing her.

For a moment, she was so dazzled she froze; then she found herself quietly enjoying the moment, and the contact. Giles kissed exactly as she'd imagined he would. With restraint and good manners. He didn't ram his tongue down her throat or maul her. He simply used his lips on hers and when she relaxed into the kiss, he deepened it. She was happily enjoying the simple kiss before she made a startling discovery. Something was happening to her. It felt as if minifireworks were going off behind her eyes—and in other parts of her body.

Maybe it had been a long time—okay, it had been a long time—for her, but she never remembered a simple kiss driving her half-crazy like this.

When he finally broke away, she realized she'd just had the perfect kiss. Not too long, not too short, not too wet, not too dry, but absolutely perfect.

She blinked hazily at him and licked her lips. They were still tingling. "What did you do that for?"

"Honestly? I did it to shut you up."

"Oh." She thought about that for a minute while a taxi vroomed by them and then a couple of guys on bikes, and the horse's bridle jingled slightly. "I talk a lot."

"You're funny. I like that about you. And you're honest, which I find frankly refreshing. You're also very beautiful, you know."

She snorted. "Yeah, I'm beautiful like—"

Shockingly, she felt Giles's hand press firmly against

her mouth. "No more putting yourself down. I insist."
He removed his hand.

"I liked it better when you kissed me to shut me up,"
she said.

"Very well," he said. And kissed her again.

They rode in the carriage barely noticing where they
went. "How can you possibly be for real?" she asked
him finally. "There has to be a catch."

"My poor, cynical Cinderella," he said, and touched
her cheek.

Before she had a chance to tell him that calling her
cynical and patting her cheek did not constitute a full
and complete answer to her question, the carriage jerked
to a stop and the driver said, "Hush Hotel, sir."

Giles paid the guy, then helped her down. Then her
date once more tucked her hand into his arm and they
walked into the hotel. The doorman nodded and greeted
them by name as he ushered them inside Hush. Sweeping in on Giles's arm, wearing her fancy gown and
shoes, she did feel like a princess in a fairy tale. Oh,
what the hell. For one weekend, why shouldn't she give
her cynical side a minivacation and free her inner princess? That's what she'd wanted, after all.

"Are you hungry?" he asked her.

"Starving," she said bluntly.

"Good," he said. "I can't bear women who pick at their
food as though it's been poisoned. I like a hearty appetite."

"Honey, you are going to love eating dinner with
me," she said, deciding that this man was definitely the
perfect stand-in Prince Charming. And if she turned
back into a stand-up comedienne come Monday, and he
turned into an extra from the latest Merchant Ivory pro-
duction, at least she'd have had a weekend to remember.

Giles was right. She had to stop looking for the trick. There was no trick. She was getting a weekend she'd longed for with all her heart. All she had to do was shut out reality for forty-eight hours and indulge.

In fact, all her appetites were hearty, but if he left her at the door to her suite with a polite kiss on the cheek, she'd still have had one of the nicest evenings of her life.

And if, come Monday, he was the part of the fantasy that turned into a pumpkin, well, she'd deal with it.

11

"DID YOU HATE the ballet very much?" Kit asked Peter. They stood close together on the Hush rooftop. When she breathed in, she caught the scent of jasmine from the garden perfuming the air. Far below hummed the incessant traffic, but up here, she felt set apart from the teeming city, closer to the stars.

"After that facial, the ballet was nothing."

He didn't sound all that upset, though. In fact, she had a sneaking feeling he'd enjoyed the ballet more than he was letting on. He came up behind her and wrapped his arms around her and she let herself lean into his strong chest and enjoy the warmth.

"You smell good," he murmured against her neck as he planted a trio of kisses at her nape.

"I think it's the flowers up here that you're smelling," she said.

"No," he mumbled against her skin, sending shivers through her, "it's definitely you."

"This is our last night," she said, feeling her body respond to his even though they'd pretty much exhausted themselves—not to mention half-drowned themselves—in the big tub earlier.

"Is it?" he asked, his lips moving to her shoulder. His breath was warm, his lips teasing.

Was it their last night? She'd been wondering that herself. Maybe there was a way to keep this incredible lover in her life. Except that letting ex-fiancés back into a woman's life seemed fraught with vague but horrendous possible complications. "I don't know," she admitted. "I have to think about it."

His lips curved against her shoulder and she felt his chuckle rumble through her. Then he raised his head and his eyes glinted down at her. "You have to plan it out, you mean. With a Venn diagram?"

His guess was close enough to what she'd been thinking that she huffed. "That's ridiculous."

"I'm seeing a white board, and several colors of pens. Purple to write down the pros of letting me back into your life. Black for the negative reasons. Yellow for neutral factors. Am I close?"

She shrugged. She wasn't about to lie. And if she'd spent some of the time he was at the spa amusing herself with a few pens and her white board, she really didn't see why she had to share that information.

"Maybe I can help you make your decision. Let's make a list now."

"That's silly. Besides, I'm hungry. Dinner will be brought up whenever we call for it."

"Indulge me."

"There's no white board up here."

"No," he said, digging into his pocket. "But I do have my PalmPilot. I can change text colors. We'll improvise."

"I can't make a list of your good and bad points with you sitting right here," she told him.

"Sure you can. I can help. Who knows my qualities and vices better than me?"

She settled herself at a black wrought-iron table. The

pool lapped quietly, reflecting the mood lighting on the roof patio and the pale wash of the moon. The man was ridiculous. She decided to call his bluff. "All right. If you want to."

"Great. I do." He opened a file. "I don't have a purple font. Pink okay?"

"Let's start with your negatives first."

She thought his shoulders slumped a little. "I hope this baby has enough memory," he said, shooting her a wry grin.

"I certainly do," she snapped.

His gaze met hers and she saw a certain eagerness. He wanted to talk about the past. Damn. She hadn't meant to sound so angry. She wasn't angry. She never dwelled on past mistakes. How odd that flash of remembered pain had felt so excruciating.

He looked as though he might say something, then seemed to think better of it. "Okay," he said, "Black font." He typed and she saw over his shoulder that he'd written a heading: Peter's Bad Points.

The curser blinked away at her as he held the small machine out. She grabbed it. Typed: Teases at inappropriate moments.

"Now you do one," she said and passed it back. He thought for a minute. Typed: Forgets to buy socks. Sometimes tries to match a black with a blue.

She read what he'd written and said, "So what? I don't care about that."

"All right then. You put down a negative thing."

She grabbed the device and typed: Pushy.

She shoved it back.

He picked it up and typed: Ran from own wedding. Bad emotional risk?

"That's not fair," she said reading the words. "If any-one was going to put that on the list, it should have been me."

"Why didn't you? It was hanging there in the atmosphere."

"Because that doesn't matter. It's over. In the past."

She went to erase his last entry but he stopped her. "Let's leave it in there for now." He glanced up. "Um, maybe we should add a few positives to this list."

"I'm really hungry. Could we eat first?"

He sighed. "All right."

She called down and, as she'd told Peter, was in-stantly assured that dinner would be sent up along with a bottle of wine personally selected by Jacob Hill.

"We call this roof service," she said, when one of the room service waiters arrived with a serving table.

No tasting menu tonight. Instead, Jacob had sent up a simple salad with organic greens and lobster ravioli. The wine was cold and crisp, and chosen by him from his native California.

"You know, I think I could live at this hotel," Peter said, as he raised his glass to hers in a silent toast.

"I know," she agreed. "I have the greatest job in the world. I spend a lot of my life here."

"So," he said, settling back in his chair, looking gor-geous and vaguely mysterious in the candlelight. "Tell me the story of your life," he said.

She wrinkled her nose in puzzlement. Tried to read his expression. "You know the story of my life," she said. "I've known you for years."

"Pretend that we met for the first time last night. Let's get to know each other."

"But that's silly." She saw him open his mouth and

raised her hand to forestall him. She knew what he was going to say. "Yeah, yeah. I know. Anything he wants."

He nodded, obviously pleased she'd guessed he was going to spout his favorite line of the weekend.

"Fine. My life story." She glanced at him and paused. How would she organize and display the facts of her life for this man if she'd just met him? What would she say? She tried to imagine he was a guy she was dating, some acquaintance of an acquaintance who'd recently moved to New York.

"I'm from Oregon originally," she began. "I was pretty good at school but not the best, a reasonable athlete, but no star. My dad's a grocery store manager, and my mother stayed home to raise us. They split up a few years ago and my mom now works for a cancer research agency. She's a fund-raiser."

"Is that who you inherited your PR talent from?" Peter asked, as though he'd never known these facts. She opened her mouth to answer and realized that no one had ever asked her that question before, including Peter.

"I don't know." She thought of her mother, so capable, maybe a little bossy and absolutely manic about how to host a dinner party. She grinned. "I guess I must have. My mother did most of her event planning as a hobby, but I'm telling you, Jacob Hill isn't better organized in the kitchen than my mom. If she cooks for a dinner party, she starts a week ahead. I'm not kidding. If dinner's on Saturday, she'll have most of the food prepared and frozen by Tuesday."

He laughed.

"No. It's true. She'll scour her place top to bottom on Thursday, lay the table on Friday, and by Saturday all she has to do is thaw the food and get dressed. I guess

I do take after her. Well, I don't freeze dinner party food ahead, of course, but I like to have everything perfect."

He sipped his wine and watched her. She had his entire attention. It was nice. "You're a long way from Oregon."

"I decided to come out east for college, mostly to get away, I guess. See something new. I met Piper at college, you know. We've been friends ever since. To tell you the truth, she wasted a lot of time at college. Not me, though. I loved it. I was born for public relations."

"What made you move to New York?" he asked. Like anyone would. As if he didn't know.

She toyed with a leaf of endive. Then put down her fork. "I was going to get married," she said. "It didn't work out."

"I'm sorry for him," Peter said, as though referring to a stranger. "But happy for me."

This was getting too weird. She sent him a brief glare. "Anyway, after I didn't end up getting married, I moved to Manhattan, got a job with a PR firm and started working my ass off. Piper hired me when she opened Hush. Like I said, it's the greatest job. Part of my responsibility is to see and be seen around town. I live a fun, single life in the greatest city in the world. What could be better?"

"What do you think you'd be doing right now if you'd married that guy in college?"

She put her chin in her hand and thought about it. Not something she'd done too much before since she wasn't big on dwelling on the past. "I don't know. He lived out of the country for a few years. If I'd married him, I probably would have lived in Hong Kong and Europe, too. Or maybe he would have got a job stateside and I'd have ended up with the same career path. Who knows?"

"Have you ever wondered if maybe it wasn't the man who was wrong, but the timing?"

"Peter, please. I do not want to go back there again."

He looked as frustrated as she felt. Why did he keep torturing her with their past?

"All right. If you won't talk about the past, then let's get back to our possible future." He drew out his PalmPilot again.

"I don't want to do that anymore. It's silly with you sitting right here."

"You can't leave a man with a list of negatives about his character and not one single positive thing. And you in public relations."

She bit back a smile. He sounded a little huffy. "I don't know."

"Just a few positives? Please?"

She held out her hand. With a cocky grin he handed the device over.

The curser blinked as she tried to come up with something positive about Peter that wouldn't end up making her sound like she still cared. She typed, watching the words come up in pink.

He read, "Good kisser." Winked at her. "All right. Let me do one." He typed and passed.

She laughed. He'd written Great in bed.

She typed Healthy Ego. Passed it over. Thank goodness they'd turned this into something fun and frivolous.

He made an entry and passed her the Palm.

There was a smile already on her face as she imagined what other boastful comment he'd come up with, but the smile froze when she read, Loves you.

She stared at the stupid pink words and fought an urge to turf his personal organizer over the balcony. She might have if she wasn't afraid it would hit somebody far below.

"You don't love me," she cried. "You never did."

She leapt to her feet, not caring any longer about hiding her hurt, and ran.

He caught her before she got to the roof exit. "I did love you. I do." He gripped her shoulders but she wouldn't look at him. She turned her head, blinking furiously.

"Please don't go. Please let me love you."

"Don't say those words." She turned to him, fierce and proud. "Don't say them."

"All right." He was trembling. She could feel it in his arms and for a second she wondered what it would be like to let herself go the way she used to, to believe in him so completely, to be so sure they'd be together forever.

To give her heart as easily as she gave her body.

"All right," he said again, "Just please, let's have this night together."

She glared at him. "And you don't love me."

He stared down at her for a long moment and then he said, "I don't love you."

He kissed her slowly, sweetly, running his hands down her back and pulling her tight against him. "I don't love the way your body fits against mine so perfectly."

He turned her so her back was to the wall. "I don't love the way your breasts feel in my hand," he said, fanning his fingers across her nipples until they ached to be touched properly.

"I don't love the way I know you so well, I can almost read your mind," he said, slipping the buttons from her midnight blue silk dress. His voice grew husky and she heard herself panting as desire tangled with emotions old and new in a fiery mix.

Proving how well he did know her, he reached for her breasts and, pushing down the silky cups of her bra, played with them in his hands until she was moaning. He kissed her feverishly. "I don't love the way you kiss me, or the taste of your nipples against my tongue," he said harshly, dropping his head to put his mouth at her breast.

"Oh," she cried, digging her fingers into his hair, holding him against her breasts while he licked and sucked at her. He scraped his teeth lightly over an engorged tip and powerful sensations shot straight to her core.

"I don't love the way the moonlight looks on your breasts," he said, baring her to the pale light that washed over the rooftop, making her skin appear milky white.

She was desperate for him, and she let him know by clawing at his shirt, anxious to get to his skin.

When she'd bared his chest and belly, he pulled her against him so their torsos rubbed back and forth.

He fumbled with his pants, and she felt his erection spring up against her belly. She whimpered with need. There was so much powerful emotion swirling around them that it seemed to channel into the one area where they had no controversy. Maybe they couldn't communicate verbally, but their bodies were dying to share with each other.

She kissed him feverishly, tasting wine and a hint of lobster, feeling his frustration even as she was certain he tasted hers. She nipped at his lower lip, let her hands clutch greedily at his hips.

He dragged her panties off and then hoisted her up, pinning her against the wall even as she wrapped her legs around him.

"And I don't love the first moment I enter you," he

said, "when I feel like everything I am and everything I'll ever be is right here."

He thrust hard and smooth, driving into her so she felt possessed and there was nothing she wanted more right at this moment. He took her hard and she reveled in it. His words were crazy, passionate, and if she wouldn't let herself believe in him again, she could respond to his lovemaking with abandon.

In fact, she couldn't help herself.

She cried out, from deep inside as he took her up and over the edge, and her cry was muffled by his mouth.

When she slid down his body and back onto her feet, she realized that nothing was different. He might think that he was in love with her, but he'd been down that road before.

So had she.

She wasn't going there again.

But, oh, how her body craved him.

"Will you come back to bed with me?" he asked, after she'd buttoned herself up and slipped her panties back on.

"Yes," she sighed, knowing they'd only just begun.

"Will you stay the night?"

"No."

12

"So, WHEN THIS WEEKEND ENDS, what happens to you?"
Irene asked Giles. They'd chatted through dinner about
all kinds of things. She might be a hick from a small
town in Ohio, but she was a passionate reader, mostly
of history and biographies. It turned out that Giles was
a bit of an amateur historian himself, so they had a lot
more in common than she'd have believed. Of course,
his family had lived a lot of the history she'd read about.

Giles sipped wine and replaced his glass. "I'll carry
on with my regular life, I suppose."

She nodded. "In England."

"Primarily, I'm based in London, of course. But I do
get over here with reasonable frequency."

"Not to Ohio, I bet."

"Not too often. You should come and visit England.
I can get you a private tour of my family estate in Kent."

"A private tour, huh. I'm impressed. You must know
people."

"A few."

She laughed. "And what would your people make
of me?"

"They'd adore you."

She snorted. "The closest thing England's ever seen
to me is Fergie. And look what happened to her."

"You aren't a bit like Fergie," he said.

"How do you know? I suppose you are personally acquainted with the royal family?"

He sent her one of those enigmatic gazes again.

She slapped a hand over her mouth. "Oh, God. I keep forgetting. I'm practically dissing your family."

"Of course, you're not." He didn't correct her about being personally acquainted, though. Wow. "Now, tell me more about your great uncle Waldo, the historian."

"He's the one who got me interested in history. He has this amazing collection of Civil War memorabilia."

"I'd love to see it sometime."

"Well, next time you're in Ohio," she said brightly.

She thought he was going to say something but he didn't. His eyes glinted at her across the intimate table width in their romantic corner of Amuse Bouche. Their expression had her pulse quickening. She'd been chatting to him so easily she'd forgotten this was a fantasy weekend date. Her fantasy. Her date.

Except, of courses, as far as he was concerned, the fantasy ended outside her fancy princess suite.

The restaurant was nearly empty, and they'd finished eating long ago. She'd probably bored him to death with all her chatter. When would she ever learn to shut up once in a while? He hadn't seemed bored, though, and he laughed at all her jokes—which she liked in a man.

"May I walk you upstairs?"

She nodded, not willing to screw anything up by speaking. He rose and then held out his hand to her. She took it, finding the palm warm and somehow sexy. She liked the way her hand fit in his. Liked the way his body seemed slightly warmer than hers.

They didn't talk as they left the restaurant, didn't

talk as they rode up in the elevator. There was a thrumming tension building between them, a feeling of inevitability in the air.

She licked her lips out of a combination of nervousness and excitement, and he watched her as intently as though she were slipping off her clothes.

When they reached her floor, the carpet seemed as buoyant as clouds as she floated along to her suite. She removed the keycard from her clutch and opened the door. Then she hesitated. Should she ask him in? Would he want to come inside, or would she only be making a fool of herself?

She glanced behind, and his eyes smoldered with intent.

Oh, the hell with making a fool of herself. Who cared? She did it all the time and with far less at stake.

"Would you like to—"

"Yes. I would," he said and walked through the doorway.

Her heart leapt. Yes. He hadn't left her at the door with a polite peck on the cheek as she'd half expected and fully dreaded. If he was here, it could only be because he was attracted to her. And of course that made her nervous, which made her a smart-ass.

"I've never done it with royalty before," she said, striving for her usual cocky attitude.

He smiled at her, and she thought he understood. He was so utterly in command of himself that she felt shaken. He was so amazing, so superior to any man she'd ever known and she could never have him for real. But it didn't matter, she reminded herself. It didn't matter if he never called because she already knew he was never going to call. He lived in friggin'

England and was next door to being a lord. She was Irene Bonnet from Ohio, who cracked jokes for a living.

"I know we only have one night," she told him. "I'm okay with that. So do me a favor and don't say things or make promises because it's what you think I want to hear. I hate that."

"All right. If that's what you want."

"It is."

He took a step closer. "May one ask, is any talking at all allowed?"

She chuckled. "Sorry. I like to be up-front is all. We only have tonight."

He moved closer still, ran a hand up her arm over her shoulder and into her hair, stroking through the thick curls until he touched her scalp. Something about the gesture was as intimate as though he'd touched her breast. "Then let's make it perfect," he said, and stepped up so their bodies touched. A shiver went through her from her head to her toe, and as she glanced up to see if he'd felt it too, he kissed her.

He kissed gently, the way he had in the carriage. He tasted her the way a connoisseur would sample the rarest vintage wine. He was a man who had all night and intended to use every minute of it.

"Yes," she whispered against his lips. "Let's make it perfect," and she led him to her big, beautiful, princess bed.

He undressed her slowly, and if he didn't make any promises, he certainly wasn't silent. His accent was so delicious, it rolled across her skin making the words almost secondary. He told her she was beautiful in ways that made her feel beautiful.

"You're so lush and ripe," he said, filling his hands with her breasts, and touching her belly and hips with delight, so she felt lush and ripe.

By contrast, his body was long and sinewy. She liked the whipcord leanness, his wonderful slim-fingered hands that looked as well cared for as her own. And oh, how those hands could touch her.

Some men were put off by her frank enthusiasm for sex. She'd wondered if Giles might be like that. Too fastidious for the noises and messes of down and dirty sex. To her surprise and delight, he loved her enjoyment of the act. Kept up with her just fine and took her over the edge more times than she'd have believed possible—even for her.

When they were both exhausted and they'd pretty much tried out every inch of her suite and played with most of the toys stored in the bedside table, they lay still. His hand played absently in her hair and her head rested on his chest.

"Did anybody ever tell you you're great in bed, your lordship?"

"I had the right partner," he said.

"No." Then she turned her head to look at him. "Really?"

"Are you fishing for a compliment?"

"Maybe a couple of little ones."

Then he whispered in her ear. "You are spectacular, earthy, with a body that was designed for sex."

"Oh, stop it. You're turning me on again."

"Well," he said, trailing a hand down her belly, "I think I could work with that."

"You really are a fantasy, aren't you?"

"No more than you are," he said, rolling on top of her and entering her with slow, lazy precision.

"I'm a fantasy? Why?"

He moved slowly, not enough to get them too worked up but enough to keep them on simmer. "You're frank. You say what you want. You care about what I want. You obviously love sex, you enjoyed playing with all the toys, but I felt that you enjoyed me as much."

"More," she sighed. "A lot more."

"Also, you talk dirty in bed and I have to say that is a rare treat for me."

"You like it?"

"Yes."

"So I shouldn't hold back?"

"Definitely not."

"Okay." She gazed up at him and she felt beautiful and sexy. So, maybe she was more of an earth mother than a princess. That was good, too.

"No toys this time?"

She shook her head. "Just us."

Then he started to move faster and she felt her body turn wild. And she didn't censor herself, not her earthy cries or her dirty talk, not her desire to explore every inch of his body or to let him discover hers. They rolled, they played, were noisy and then, at the end, very quiet, as they held each other through the sweetest of all fantasies. Mutual pleasure.

With a sigh, she rolled to her side and he curled his body around hers, one hand slipping to her breast. She fell asleep with the feel of his palm warm above her heart and the sound of his breathing soft in her ear.

IRENE WOKE WITH A SMILE on her face. A stupid, goofy, oh-I-never-knew-it-could-be-like-that grin. She rolled over to see if Giles was awake yet, and the grin froze.

He was gone.

There was a dent in the second pillow that proved he had been there, but of the man himself not a sign.

Well, she should be used to it by now. Men left her bed in the night sometimes. Nature of the beast. She shrugged, trying to convince herself that the hollow feeling in her belly was hunger. Or caffeine withdrawal.

She'd had a great, incredible, fantastic night. She had had no right to expect anything. In fact, she hadn't. She'd been so busy telling him that she didn't have any expectations beyond last night, why the hell hadn't she listened to all those tough words she'd spouted?

The trouble with fantasies, she realized as she dragged herself out of bed, was that they were meant to be dreamed, not lived. What happened to a person who lived a fantasy? Were they forever changed? Would she now spend the rest of her life trying to find a man who could make her feel the way Sir Giles had made her feel for one special night?

She groaned. Coffee. Everything would be better once she'd had some coffee.

And maybe he'd left her a note somewhere. She could imagine it.

Dear Irene,
Thank you for a lovely evening. Unfortunately, Her Majesty requires my urgent attendance at Buckingham Palace.
Sincerely,
The Honorable Giles Pendleton.

Oh, well. He was gone. It didn't really matter.

As though her intense craving had conjured it, she caught the scent of fresh coffee.

Okay, so she'd put the in-room pot on and then shower.

She padded toward the bathroom and then jumped a mile when the door opened and Giles stepped out.

"Giles!" She wanted to run to him and throw her arms around him. He hadn't left. He'd been in the shower. He was wearing nothing but a towel and staring at her in a way that reminded her of every single thing they'd done last night.

Only then did it hit her that she was naked.

And it was morning. The suite was full of unforgiving light and Giles stared at her as though he wanted to start last night all over again.

"I love the way you look," he said.

Oh, so she wasn't perfect. Maybe a little rounder than she'd like. If he liked the way she looked who was she to argue? Instead of cracking cellulite jokes, she smiled at him and said, "Thanks."

"I made you coffee."

She wanted to laugh. She wanted to cry. She wanted to fall at his feet and beg him to be real. "Mmm. Wonderful."

He poured her a mug and she took it gratefully, drinking several scalding sips. "I can't believe you made me coffee."

"While you're drinking it, I need to ask your advice about something." He sounded so serious she drank some more coffee. The more caffeine in her system, the better she could cope with whatever he wanted to talk about. His wife and eleven children? The fact that he was on the run from an international crime syndicate? How he needed to check in with his psychiatrist or parole officer?

"Okay," she said, taking one more jolt of coffee. "What do you want to ask me?"

"Can you please explain the purpose of this?" he asked, picking up a red plastic object shaped a little like an octopus.

It was obviously one of the sex toys that Hush stocked, but he showed it to her with the same concentrated expression as though he'd discovered a new life form.

She tried to keep the grin off her face but couldn't quite succeed.

"Tell you what," she said, "I need to shower and brush my teeth. While I'm doing that maybe you can dream up some ways to use that thing."

He turned it upside down, around, peered at it from all sides. "It has me in a puzzle."

"You are too cute," she said, giving him a quick kiss on her way past him.

Well, she thought, as she rubbed wonderful scented liquid soap on her body, it seemed that her magical night was spilling over into a magical day.

And she simply wouldn't think about tomorrow.

13

PETER FINALLY TRACKED KIT down in the hotel lobby, chatting to one of the guests as though she was working on the weekend instead of fulfilling one very demanding contest winner's every fantasy.

Since his fantasy weekend was going to be over in about three hours, he walked smack up to Kit and some L.A.-looking hot shot who obviously had ideas about Kit that were not going to become reality.

"Hi, babe," he said, kissing her cheek. "Sorry to keep you waiting."

Her annoyance was evident in the quick glare she sent him before showing her PR face to Mr. L.A. "I know you're going to love Hush," she said, holding out her hand.

"Honey, I already do," he said, and with a nod to Peter he walked away.

"Don't you ever do anything like that again," Kit said in a furious undertone.

"But it's the weekend. You're not even wearing your name tag."

"That's not the point. I have a position of respect in this hotel that doesn't include kissing the guests."

"You did a lot more than kiss me last night," he reminded her.

"But that was in private."

They probably would have stood there arguing all day if they hadn't been hailed. Irene and Giles were walking toward them. Irene looked a little less the princess and a lot more the stand-up comic today, but at least she was wearing some of the more subdued of the items that Kit had seen in her closet. If you didn't count the bright red Keds on her feet.

Giles, as perfectly put together as ever, said, "We were just going to have breakfast. Care to join us?"

"We'd love to," said Peter before Kit could open her mouth. He knew perfectly well that she'd try to fob him off if she got the chance.

She tried. "I've already—"

"Anything he wants," Peter reminded her with a grin that hid his disappointment.

She'd left him again some time in the night. He'd woken alone, knowing this was the last morning of his magic weekend and he was no nearer getting Kit back than he had been Friday morning.

He'd tried calling Giles, just for somebody to bounce his troubles off of, but Giles must have been in the pool or something because he hadn't answered.

He needed to figure out some kind of plan to show Kit that he'd changed, that he'd grown up, that he was ready for her now. He had to show her that his love was real and permanent. And he had an awful feeling he had to do it fast.

"All right," said Kit, and he was pathetically grateful.

When they got into the restaurant and they'd finished ordering, Peter said to Giles, "So, were you working out this morning?"

He got an enigmatic look in return. "No."

"I tried to call you but there was no answer in your room."

"*Peter,*" Kit said in that *shut up* tone women use when they think you're being indiscreet.

"I wasn't in my room," Giles explained.

"But where—"

Even as Kit kicked him under the table, Giles said, "A gentleman doesn't tell."

"He was in my room," Irene said in a smug tone that suggested Giles hadn't bunked in the spare bedroom.

Peter felt suddenly that nothing in his world made sense anymore. "You slept with Irene?"

"Peter!" Kit said, looking like she wanted to smack him.

Peter barely acknowledged her outrage. He was staring at his old friend. "But you're—"

"What?" Irene asked, pausing before sipping her coffee to raise her brows at him. "Are there more secrets I should know about? If he's not in banking, I can deal with it. Not being royalty will be a little tougher, but I think I can learn to live with that. So, unless Giles is married or his prison weekend pass is about to expire, you probably can't shock me too much."

Ha. That's what she thought. God this was more awkward than he'd have believed possible. "Well, Giles is… I mean, it was clear this didn't have to be a sex thing, and Kit was desperate."

"Thanks a lot," Irene said.

"No, I don't mean that, I mean… I always thought, everyone thinks…"

"Thinks what?" Irene insisted.

He glanced at Giles looking for some help, but the Englishman simply regarded him with mild, and irritatingly amused, interest.

Well, there was no graceful way out of what he'd

blundered into and besides, Irene had a right to know. "Giles is gay."

Irene laughed. Then she slapped her hand over her mouth but that only made the giggles sound like snorts.

Giles cut a perfect square of omelet and put it into his mouth.

When Irene had stopped laughing, she said, "He's not gay. He's English. Sometimes with those snotty types, it's hard to tell the difference."

Peter had never been that wrong about anybody, except maybe when he had run off and left Kit. He couldn't be that far off base. "Are you..." He flapped his hand from side to side.

"Am I?" Giles leaned forward with his brows raised and a question mark hovering in the air.

"I think he wants to know if you're bisexual," Irene said helpfully.

"My goodness. What very odd topics you do choose for the breakfast table, Peter," Giles said.

"Well, are you?"

Giles took a napkin and patted his mouth. He glanced at Irene and the way they looked at each other pretty much sizzled the table linen. "No, Peter. I'm not. I'm as straight as you are."

"But you enjoyed that facial, I swear you did."

"You would have, too, if you didn't spend the entire afternoon fighting off some implied threat to your masculinity."

Kit didn't say anything to defend him. First, she'd seemed shocked at his suggestion that his old friend was gay and now, based on the ill-concealed grin on her face, she was enjoying his discomfort.

He ought to drop the subject, but somehow he felt

that this was all part of his problem. Could his sense of people suck that badly?

"How come I've never seen you with a woman, then? I mean before this weekend."

"We've never really socialized all that much, you know. It's been business lunches and things."

"You've seen me with women. And I always assumed you never got married because—"

"I was gay. Yes. You've made that clear."

Giles stirred his coffee slowly, as though debating something. Then he looked up, not at Peter or Kit, but at Irene.

"I had a...close friendship with a woman for many years. She was in an unhappy marriage, but wouldn't leave her husband or children. We were utterly discreet. I'd have married her if I could, but it wasn't possible." He sounded so sad. Irene put her hand over his.

"What happened?"

"She died," he said softly. "Car accident. Stupid bloody car accident."

"When?"

"Four years ago." He smiled briefly. "In our way, we were faithful to each other for twenty years."

"Oh, honey, I'm sorry."

He gripped her hand and it was as if they'd forgotten they weren't alone. "You made me laugh again, Irene."

Peter wished he were miles away. Or at least that he'd kept his fool mouth shut.

Then Giles turned back to his coffee and it was clear he'd revealed as much as he was going to. Wow. Peter had always though Giles was a cool customer, but he'd never realized how much he hadn't known.

"So, I was totally and completely wrong about you," Peter said.

"I'm afraid so."

He narrowed his eyes. His people judgment might suck, but he wasn't totally stupid. "You knew what I thought, though, didn't you?"

A slight smile flickered across that aristocratic countenance. "Yes. I had my suspicions."

"Why didn't you ever say anything?"

"First, because I'm not usually in the habit of discussing my personal life, and second, because it did you a great deal of good to presume you had a gay man as a friend."

"But...but...I'm sure there's some logic buried in there somewhere, I don't know what it is, though."

"I'm sorry, Irene," Kit said suddenly. "I had no idea when Peter suggested Giles that—"

"Hey, it's okay. Turned out pretty good for me." She beamed at her new lover. "I'm having a great fantasy weekend."

Damn it, this wasn't going at all the way he'd hoped. Soon he'd have to leave and he had no idea how to get Kit back. His old business acquaintance was clearly not only straight but great at getting women to fall at his feet. Look at Funny Girl, there. She looked more like a dreamy bride than the smart mouth of yesterday. Giles, *Giles,* who'd fooled him for years, wasn't even gay, and he was great with women, while Peter who'd always had a way with women couldn't get any commitment from the woman he loved to even see him again. The world was a stranger place by the minute.

"So, Giles," he said, "What are you up to later today?" He was going to have to find some time to pick the man's brains for advice.

Giles raised his thin eyebrows. "We're going to catch up with some light reading in the library," he said, then shot a glance at his date that suggested reading wasn't going to be a big part of the day's activity.

"But we have to check out today," Peter reminded him.

"Not us," Irene told him. "I had to start my weekend late so they extended me until tomorrow." She glanced coquettishly at the man sitting beside her. "Giles is staying to keep me company."

"Oh." Peter turned to Kit with renewed hope. Maybe if he could stay another day, too, then he could impress her with his desire to renew their relationship. "Do you think I could stay another night, too?"

"Sorry, dude. Your fantasy weekend ends at noon." She glanced at her watch. "About an hour from now."

"But I could—"

"The suite's booked for tonight, and most of the regular rooms are gone."

Okay, so she didn't want him hanging around. He got her incredibly unsubtle message. She was probably lying about the hotel occupancy, that's how badly she wanted him out. "It was a stupid idea anyway. I have to work tomorrow."

Giles and Irene ate rapidly, clearly anxious to get on with the day's program. Peter tried not to notice that they were playing footsie under the table while he and Kit preserved a perfectly respectable distance. He wanted to play footsie under the table, too, but he could see from Kit's expression that all he'd get if he tried to initiate a round would be a shoeful of squished toes.

An odd feeling seemed to expand beneath his ribs, putting him off his food. It took him a few minutes to realize it wasn't indigestion, but panic. What would he do if he couldn't get Kit back?

But that was ridiculous. Of course he was going to get her back. He needed to stop playing games—they both needed to stop playing games. He'd lost this woman once. He didn't plan to lose her again.

When Giles and Irene had bolted down the last bit of sex fuel on their plates, which they clearly planned to burn off in pretty short order, Giles said, "Well, I hate to eat and run, but…"

Irene was already on her feet. "If I don't see you again, Peter, it was nice to meet you," she said holding out her hand. She smiled at him and he could have sworn he saw pity in her eyes. He had a moment's horror that he'd end up as the punch line in one of her stand-up routines. Then she leaned forward and kissed his cheek. "Good luck," she whispered.

"Thanks. You, too," he whispered back. Then she and Giles were gone as fast as their oversexed bodies could carry them.

Leaving him, Kit, and four cups of coffee in varying degrees of coolness and emptiness.

"Well," Kit said, with that PR expression back on her like impregnable Happy Face armor, "I'd better get moving. I've got a lot to do today."

He put a hand on her arm. "My weekend isn't up until noon."

"Peter," she said, sounding totally exasperated, "That's less than an hour from now. What possible fantasy can you fulfill in—" she glanced at her yellow Happy Face watch "—forty-seven minutes?"

"I can talk to you, and I intend to."

She rolled her eyes and settled her elbows on the table and her chin into her hands with an expression of spurious interest. "Okay, talk."

"Not here," he said. "I want your undivided attention—"

"You have my undivided attention."

"And privacy."

She let out an annoyed sigh. "Oh, fine. Let's get this over with."

She rose and he followed. "Where to?" she snapped.

"My room."

She looked as though she was going to argue, then just shrugged. "Fine."

There was silence as they rode the elevator to the sixteenth floor. Silence as they trod the plush carpet to the door of his suite. Silence so thick his keycard sounded deafening as he gained entrance.

It was a little lame, he knew, to bring her here hoping the memories of their recent passion would soften her up enough to listen to him, but he was desperate enough to try anything.

Kit walked in ahead of him and her gaze immediately swiveled to the bed. As did his. Her obvious relief that the efficient Hush maids had already been in and made the bed was exactly equivalent to his level of irritation at the same efficiency.

He'd wanted her to see the rumpled sheets and dented pillows that were intimate reminders of their lovemaking. Instead, everything was as smooth and impersonal as Kit was trying to act.

Couldn't anything go his way this morning?

Kit seemed as though she didn't know where to move, so she stood in the middle of the room. Even though the bed was made and everything neat and cleaned, he hoped that when she glanced at the jetted tub she'd see steamy images of their soap-slicked bodies, as he did, or that when she saw the bed, she would be reminded of the way they'd used every single inch of it last night.

"Kit," he said, "I want to talk to you."

"Well, for the next forty-three minutes, I'm listening."

"Look, explaining my feelings isn't easy for me." He tried a grin on her. "The full fruit facial and pedicure is a snap compared to trying to tell you what I feel."

"Then maybe you shouldn't bother."

He sat on the edge of the bed and pulled out his wallet. He opened it as he'd done thousands of times over the last three years, and he carefully slipped the photograph out that he'd stared at so often. He passed it over to Kit.

She walked over and took the photograph he held out. It was a little bent from its years in his wallet, but still in pretty good shape. She stared at the photograph for a long, silent moment. Her hand trembled slightly, and then suddenly she dropped to sit on the bed beside him.

"Where did you get this?" Her voice was strained and low.

"Piper sent it to me."

"Why would she do something to me that cruel?"

"I think it was me she was hoping to punish, not you."

"I look so young."

They stared at the photo of a younger, carefree Kit smiling joyfully at the camera on her wedding day. "You look so happy."

"You should have seen me an hour later," she said.

"I know," he said, staring at her profile. "I should have. An hour later, and a day later and every day from then until now."

Kit seemed to snap out of the spell the photo had cast over her. "It wasn't meant to be, Peter. Our marriage would have been a disaster."

She turned the photo onto its side and he caught her the second he realized her intention was to rip the picture in two. "No," he said, taking it away from her.

"It is really sick to keep the picture of a jilted bride in your wallet. What is that? Some kind of trophy?"

"It's my penance." He stared down at that loving, happy face. "I thought when I came here this weekend that I could talk to you and make sure that you were okay with the way your life had turned out. That you were happier without me. Then I was going to tear up this picture and let go of the guilt I've been carrying around for three years."

She held out her hand, palm flat. "Then let's do it. Right now. I want to rip that thing to pieces. I'm fine. I'm happy. Go off and have a great life."

He shook his head. "I said that's what I thought I wanted. But I was wrong." He stared into her eyes, those summer-blue eyes that he'd always loved. They were cold and hard now, but he loved those eyes in all their moods. He touched her thigh where it nudged his on the bed. "I never should have run out on you. Kit, I'm sorry."

Like a sudden storm had come in, the cold blue of her eyes turned dark and cloudy. She suddenly leapt off the bed and marched to stare out the window. Anger vibrated from every line of her body.

"Sorry?" she yelled the word so it echoed back at him off the windows. "You're sorry? You want to know what it was like? You've been needling me all weekend to tell. Okay. Fine. I'll tell you. There were two hundred pounds of salmon flown in fresh from British Columbia. Wild sockeye. My dad bought twenty cases of vintage champagne. He supervised the chilling of the wine himself.

"The flowers were just opening. I have never seen such perfect roses."

She took a quick breath, the kind of breath he knew meant she wanted to cry but wouldn't let herself. "And there was me. Standing there feeling so happy, and then nervous, and then terrified something had happened to you. That you'd got sick or been in an accident. And then, much later, I guess I accepted the truth. That you had run off and abandoned me. For a long time after that, I hated the smell of roses."

"I remember those roses," he said.

"You never saw them."

"I remember you got obsessed about the color. Pink, but not too pink. A little yellow around the edges would be good, but nothing too egg yolky." It had been a nightmare. Had he tried to talk to her about his increasing panic? Probably not. It seemed she had been incapable of talking about anything but wedding planning details anyway. But if he had tried to explain that he'd said he loved her, not that he wanted to marry her before they had even graduated college, he doubted she would have heard.

"I wanted everything to be perfect," she said.

"I never saw you." He shook his head. "For months. You were so busy with the wedding of the century that you never had a second to spare for the fun we'd been having up until then. Even our sex life went to shit."

He remembered one vivid night when he'd come to her place bagged to find a dozen boutonnieres laid out on her desk. "Pick one," she'd said. It was like picking one beer over another in the same case—every one of them was a single rose with some green crap. Who cared which one?

Instead of making love that night as he'd hoped, they'd had a stupid fight about how he didn't even care about the flowers for his own wedding.

Damn straight he hadn't. Then he'd gone to her closet to change his shoes and she'd screamed at him. Her dress was in there. He wasn't allowed to see it before the wedding day. Bad luck.

"I don't even know what you're talking about. Everything was fine. Maybe I was a little busy, since I did so much of the wedding planning myself, but you saw me all the time."

"If you weren't off getting fitted for the dress or driving a hundred miles to see if you could find fresher flowers, you were so busy obsessing about place cards that we might as well not have been in the same room."

She swung around. "You could have said something, instead of taking the coward's way out."

He rose and took a step closer, only one because the way she was standing there, vibrating with emotion, one more step was going to have her running out that door. "I thought I was going to my wedding. I had my tux on, and my boutonniere. I swear to God, I didn't consciously plan to miss the wedding. I was rehearsing my toast to whoever I was supposed to toast—"

"The bridesmaids," she supplied.

"Right. I was rehearsing my speech and I missed the turnoff for the country club. No problem, I figured. I'd turn around at the next intersection."

There was a pause while they stared at each other, both recalling that awful day.

"I stood there, in front of two hundred guests, some of whom had flown miles. At first, we joked about you being late. Then everyone started to get real quiet and they sent me these looks of pity." She wrapped her arms around herself.

"Our friends. My friends. My mother and my father. The minister." She laughed, an unamused laugh. "He had another wedding to do that afternoon. He kept looking at his watch when he thought I didn't see him. And you know what's really sad?"

He shook his head.

"I still believed in you. I really thought you would come. He loves me, I thought. Peter would never, ever do this to me."

She was crying now, the tears she'd bottled up so long spilling freely down her cheeks.

"I'm so sorry," he said, the words sounding feeble and inadequate. He tried to take her into his arms, but she pushed him away.

"This is ridiculous," she said, swiping her hands over her wet cheeks. She glanced at her watch. "And time's up, anyway. Goodbye, Peter."

She walked toward the door.

"Wait," he said.

She turned, looking sad and impatient at the same time. "What is it now?"

"Maybe it's too late, but you have to know how I feel. I made the biggest mistake of my life when I ran away that day. Please, please give me another chance."

"How could I ever trust you again?"

"I… Look at Irene. She trusts Giles, and that's a hell of a lot more of a stretch. She's letting herself believe that her Cinderella fantasy is going to come true." He shook his head. "And the crazy thing is that it's happening. Maybe that happy-ending thing can happen again for us."

The noise she made was somewhere between a snort of derision and a hiccup. "Goodbye, Peter."

"Kit, I love you."

She looked less than impressed. Her brows rose and the corners of her mouth turned down.

He smiled at her, feeling sad and hopeless. "The last time I told you I loved you, you immediately started planning the wedding."

"Well, believe me, our wedding is one event I will never again plan."

Without another word or so much as a glance in his direction, she left. The door took its sweet time closing, and he watched it all the way.

14

KIT COULD BARELY SEE, which infuriated her. She never cried. And she never, ever, ever cried over a man.

Not anymore.

There was a package of novelty Happy Face tissues in her bag but, naturally, she didn't have her bag when she needed it. So she sniffed and wiped her eyes with the heels of her hands and disappeared into the stairwell so as not to have to bump into any guests. She needed to get out, and fast. No way she was hanging around while Peter was in the hotel. She ran all the way down the stairs to her office, grabbed her bag, blew her nose defiantly into a Happy Face tissue and then bolted.

She ran for the employee entrance off the lower level, planning to disappear into the closest subway station on Lexington Avenue and ride home. But she never made it to the exit. A low, throaty laugh caught her attention. She'd know that sound anywhere.

Without pausing for a nanosecond's thought, she walked into Piper's office. "You're back early," she said, and then stopped dead, color rushing to her face. "Oh, Piper, Trace. I'm sorry,"

No wonder Piper was giggling. She'd be giggling, too, if the man she loved had her on her back on her desk. They were fully clothed, but five minutes later they wouldn't have been. Already Trace had slid the strap of Piper's low-cut dress off her shoulder and his mouth was busy.

Kit turned to flee, only to have Piper's voice stop her. "No, Kit. Don't go." Then a grunt. "Get off me, Trace. We'll finish this later."

"Oh, honey, yes we will." Trace planted one more smacking kiss somewhere while Kit kept her face averted, then he strolled past and winked at Kit. "Next time knock, kid."

"Oh, God, I'm sorry," Kit said, dropping to the couch.

Piper rose to sit as gracefully as a cat, then swiveled her butt so she was facing Kit, her legs crossed at the ankles and hanging off the desk. Her upper chest gleamed with moisture from where Trace had been kissing her. She had that freshly laid look, but then Piper had pretty much had that look going on since she was a teenager. "Don't worry about it. A little anticipation is good for a man."

Kit crawled onto the floor and retrieved two pens and a staple remover that had been knocked to the floor in Piper's latest round of inappropriate office behavior.

"You should put all your office supplies on bungee cords," Kit muttered.

Piper laughed and nonchalantly pulled her strap back onto her shoulder. "You look like hell. What's going on?"

"Don't give me that innocent look. You know exactly what's going on." Anger spurted through her body. "You should have told me the winner was Peter. You should have told me. And how *convenient* that Cassie didn't show after I'd confirmed with her that very morning. You did more than hide Peter's identity from me."

"Yeah. You're right. For the record, Cassie didn't

want to let you down. I bribed her with a screen test with a friend of mine in L.A. A hot young producer. I also promised she'd still get the bonus and another crack at being a fantasy weekend hostess." Piper looked troubled. "I figured I was doing you both a favor. When you called and interrupted me and Trace on Saturday night, I got pretty pleased with myself. The way you were talking, it seemed like there was a lot of good stuff going on between you and Peter. I imagined that one day we'd laugh about this."

"I'm not laughing, Piper."

"Okay. Let's take this from the top. You showed up at his suite looking like a million bucks. Had a great dinner. He gave you a list of things he wanted to do that was really a schedule of your perfect day. Then I went to the Hamptons." She put her palms back on the desk and shook her hair off her shoulders, Playboy centerfold-style. Piper had practiced vamping so long it was second nature now. "What did I miss?"

"A few awkward conversations and some pretty amazing sex."

"Get out!"

"Yeah, well. It was a stupid idea."

"Which? The talking or the amazing sex?"

"Both."

Piper shook her hair again so that it rippled in a sexy fall. "Tell me all about the sex first. Details."

Kit found a scrunchie and tied her hair back into a neat ponytail. She was still angry with Piper for deceiving her, but right now she needed to accept that Piper had, in her misguided way, meant the best. And she needed her friend's advice. Or maybe her pampered shoulder to cry on. "The sex was kind of like before, only better."

"Really? Even after three years in Manhattan?"

Kit nodded miserably.

"He's still the best you've ever had?"

Desperately she scanned her list of lovers. Surely someone had out-wowed him in the bedroom. At last, she nodded again.

"Cool."

"He told me he loved me."

"No way! When?"

"About fifteen minutes ago."

"In bed or out of bed?"

Kit rolled her eyes. "Out."

Piper straightened. They'd played these games so many times. "Clothes or no clothes?"

"Clothes."

"Okay. He means it."

"No, he doesn't. He came here looking for me to blame him for ruining my life. I swear he was disappointed when he saw I'm fine. I'm over him."

A disbelieving snort was her answer. Kit chose to ignore it.

"The minute he figured out I'm fine and have a great life, he started chasing after me." She shook her head in disgust. "Men."

"Why'd you sleep with him?"

"For the same reason you usually sleep with guys." She smiled slightly. "Used to sleep with guys. I felt like it."

"And you wanted to prove to him you could screw him and leave him."

Kit dropped her head in her hands. "I didn't think of it in those terms, but that probably had something to do with it. That was sort of clichéd of me, wasn't it?"

"Not as sucky a cliché as Peter pulled. The old leaving the bride at the altar thing is getting stale."

In spite of her misery, Kit laughed. Trust Piper to expect a trendier breakup. "You're right. He should have sent me a bouquet of dead roses with a drop dead-o-gram."

"Or he could have had his matching tattoo removed."

"We never had tattoos."

"You were smart. Hurts like hell when you get them lasered off." Piper seemed to wince.

"I guess."

"You know, one reason we're still friends is you never remind me that you warned me not to get Rock's name tattooed on my ass. Okay. This is as good a segue as any. I sort of thought I was helping you get Peter out of your skin. Did it help at all? Seeing him again? Having a chance to talk about stuff?"

"I don't know. I feel really churned up right now. He made me so mad. He showed me a picture of me you sent him," she glared at Piper. "Which you never told me you'd done."

"Bastard. I wanted him to see what he was missing." She glanced up and opened her eyes wide. "He still has it?"

"He keeps it in his wallet."

"Interesting."

"Sick. I tried to tear it up, but he wouldn't let me." She let out a breath. "So he showed me this picture and started apologizing again. I looked down at that picture of myself and suddenly it was like I was there again, you know? With the smell of roses all around me and two hundred guests all dressed up waiting for 'Here Comes the Bride.'"

"Instead, they got 'There Goes the Groom.'"

"Yeah. And I lost it. I told him what it was like. The humiliation. And you know what he said?" Her voice rose but she couldn't seem to stop it.

"What?"

"He said he hated picking boutonnieres."

The phone on Piper's desk rang but she ignored it.

"You made him pick boutonnieres?"

"Of course I did. They were for the groomsmen. I wanted them to be perfect. I wanted everything to be perfect."

"He said he didn't show up because of some friggin' carnation for his lapel?"

"Rosebud. Cream, white or oyster. With a choice of greenery." She shook her head. "No. That's not why he left. He said he never saw me because I was planning the wedding and...oh, it's stupid."

Piper slid off the desk and came to sit beside Kit. "Maybe he was trying to tell you something important."

"Piper," she warned, "if you quote anyone who appears on daytime television..."

"No. I'm not going to." She grinned slyly. "But I did read this book where this—I don't know—psychologist or psychiatrist or something said that you should say what you mean and mean what you say."

"That should change the future of self-help as we know it."

"No, but listen. If Peter was trying to say what he meant, you know, deep down, that serious stuff that guys can never say...maybe he freaked because of you planning the wedding so perfectly."

Kit got up and stalked across the room. "What are you implying? If we'd taken the bus to city hall some lunch hour that we'd be celebrating our leather anniversary?"

"Leather anniversary?"

Kit turned. "The third wedding anniversary. The traditional gift is leather. The modern equivalent is crystal or glass."

"You sure know a lot of weird facts." Piper shifted on the couch. "But the point is that Peter was trying to tell you why he cut and ran."

"If he didn't want to marry me because I wanted the boutonnieres to be perfect, then he didn't deserve me."

"Of course he didn't deserve you." Piper drew a noisy breath, as if she had something difficult to say. "But you can get a little carried away sometimes."

Kit blinked at her.

Piper stared back steadily. "Life isn't perfect, Kit. I've screwed up enough of mine to know that. You know what I think?"

"That I should say what I mean and mean what I say?"

"Yes. But besides that, I think your parents' divorce screwed you up more than you ever let on. You had this perfect life and then suddenly it blasted apart. It's like your mom planned this perfect life and it blew up on her, so you are determined to do a better job so life can't blow up in your face."

"But it always does."

"I read in this book that we either copy our parents' marriage because that's how we learned about marriage or we deliberately do something different. So my theory about you is that you wanted the perfect family life without the mistakes your parents made. You planned the wedding so perfectly, you forgot about what Peter wanted."

Kit felt a little sick, as though there wasn't enough air in the room. If there'd been a window down here, she'd have opened it. "You're my best friend. How can you blame me for my fiancé leaving me at the altar?"

"I don't blame you. I'm saying, maybe Peter's trying to tell you something important."

"You think I try too hard."

"It's a pattern. It's the same with your job. Nobody does better promotions than you. Nobody in town has your imagination and flair. But sometimes you go a teensy bit overboard."

"The crocodiles," she breathed.

"Kind of a metaphor for your life."

"I don't believe in dwelling on the negative things in my past."

"How can you learn from mistakes if you ignore them?"

"Peter was the biggest mistake I ever made."

"Then learn from him."

Kit stared blindly at her friend for a moment. "I have to go."

"Call me."

She flapped her hand behind her, which she hoped Piper would take as a possible yes, but maybe not. She didn't think she could handle any more pop psychology today.

She paid no attention to where she was going, following the stream of traffic to the subway on Lexington Avenue. She made her way home on autopilot and stumbled into her apartment. She'd had barely any sleep in the last two days; that must be why she felt so peculiar.

She got out her vitamins. The special health food store brand for active women, the extra B complex, and the calcium because she was already protecting her bones from osteoporosis.

She wasn't hungry, but she felt she needed something comforting, so she brewed some tea and put it in a pretty china mug.

Then she sat down in her easy chair in her small living room. No music, no TV, no distractions of any kind. And she started thinking.

Was Piper right? Had Peter been trying to tell her that she'd scared him away with her over-the-top wedding plans?

So, he carried her wedding-day picture around and talked a good line about being sorry. His behavior was still inexcusable.

Now he was telling her he loved her?

What kind of man walked away from the woman he loved?

What kind of woman was so obsessed with perfection that she drove her man away?

Suddenly a mental image flashed across her mind of her as a child. She was trying to tell her mother about some minor accomplishment at school. She was having milk and cookies and in her excitement was waving the cookie around. Between reminding her not to chew with her mouth open and wiping up the crumbs, her mother had barely heard a word she'd said.

At least her mom had been married for fifteen years before she drove Kit's father away. Kit hadn't even made it through the wedding ceremony.

Okay, so Peter had done a terrible, unforgivable thing. But, for the first time in three years, she realized that she'd played a role in the disaster of her wedding.

Was Piper right? Did she keep setting herself up?

She reviewed some of her recent promotions. She

was edgy, that's all, she thought. People loved her promotions. But there was always that feeling that she teetered on the edge of disaster.

15

"I HOPE YOU ENJOYED your stay here at Hush, Mr. Garson," the front desk receptionist said to him when he turned in his keycard. There was a little smile that went with the comment—the sort that suggested he'd be a damned fool or a monk in training if he didn't have a great time at Hush.

"One of the best weekends of my life," he assured her, startled to realize that was the truth. He'd wasted too many weekends and weekdays and years without Kit. Starting this weekend, he had really hoped he could convince her that he deserved a second chance.

Naturally, the woman he wished to beg the second chance from was nowhere near the vicinity of the front desk.

"Our limousine is available to take you anywhere in the city," the desk clerk said.

"Thanks. I may take you up on it, but I have something to do first."

"Certainly, sir. Let me know when you're ready to leave and I'll let the driver know."

He hooked his overnight bag over his shoulder and went back to the elevator. He wanted to say goodbye properly. He hadn't done such a smooth job of it earlier. Maybe Kit was in her office.

When he got to the lower level, though, it was pretty quiet. He walked by Kit's office, but the lights were dimmed, her computer off. Nobody home.

He was about to head back to the lobby when a female voice said, "Well, well. There's a face from the past."

He turned and there was Piper, as gorgeous and sultry as ever. She was looking at him quizzically. Friend or foe? He couldn't tell which she was right now.

He decided to go on the assumption that she was his friend, until she kicked him in the balls or in some other very direct way let him know she was the opposite. He smiled broadly. "Hey, Piper. Looking good."

She let him approach, let him kiss her cheek and refrained from kicking him. So far so good.

"Thanks for helping me get some time with Kit this weekend."

"As I told Kit, when she chewed out my ass for the same thing, I couldn't have done anything if your fantasy hadn't spoken to her." Piper regarded him. "You got to her."

"Yeah. I know." He puffed his cheeks and blew out his frustration. "But not enough for her to give me another chance at being part of her life."

"What did you expect?"

He dragged a hand through his hair. "Honestly? I expected closure. And then I saw her again."

"And?"

He glanced at Piper. She looked truly interested. "And I felt like somebody had let the air out of my lungs. She's amazing, incredible, more beautiful than ever and—"

"And you broke her heart."

"She pretends she's over me."

"Of course she's over you. Did you think she was going to sit by the phone for three years?" She laughed, but not unkindly. "But it doesn't mean she doesn't still have feelings for you."

"I'm ready now, in a way I wasn't ready before. Kit is the love of my life, as corny as that sounds, but I guess I was too young to realize it."

"Poor timing."

"Yeah. The thing is, now that the weekend's over, I don't know what to do. She doesn't want to see me anymore."

"Did she say so?"

"Not in so many words, but the rejection was implied."

Piper turned. "Come on into my office." She didn't bother to see if he was following, but turned and walked with her model's gait into a doorway farther down the hall.

He followed and entered a comfortable but not exactly swank office.

"You look surprised."

"I expected leopard skin rugs and a private martini bar," he admitted.

She laughed. "I keep all that stuff upstairs, for the paying guests. Down here, we work."

She settled herself in the chair behind her desk, loan officer-style, and he settled on a deep leather couch, which put him lower and at a definite disadvantage. He could stand up, but he had a feeling she enjoyed having the upper hand and right now he'd do anything for her cooperation, including looking up at her.

"So," she said, tossing her hair over her shoulder with one manicured finger, "you want to see Kit."

"Yes." Not a real stretch there.

"And she doesn't want to see you."

"I don't know that for sure. But it was implied."

Piper pondered the problem for a few moments then grinned and leaned forward. "She'll see you if it's about business."

"You think I should check into the hotel? I've already got an apartment."

"No, I don't think you should check into the hotel. What good would that do? Kit's not on the reservation desk. She's not a chambermaid."

"Right. She's in PR."

"Uh-huh." She looked at him as though he were supposed to guess what was coming next. He couldn't so she went on. "And Kit does all our in-house special events."

"Right."

"What is your new job?"

"I'm sales director for a New-York-based international marketing firm."

"And, probably the sales director for an international marketing firm might want to put on—oh, I don't know—some kind of big event to mark his arrival? Maybe a customer appreciation evening, or a launch of some product?" She leaned forward a little more. "You see where I'm going with this?"

"You think I should create an event so I can use the services of Hush?"

She smiled. "Seems like a swell idea to me."

"And the fact that your hotel would get a nice bit of business never crossed your mind."

"Let's call it a win-win situation."

"You don't think that's a little manipulative?"

She opened her eyes wide. "More manipulative than entering a contest to see your former fiancée?"

He had to grin. "An event that would introduce me to a lot of movers and shakers. Kind of a splashy do that would be totally different from the usual. It's not a bad idea. I'll think about it."

He rose. She stood and walked around her desk to join him. "Here," she said and handed him a folder with the Hush logo on it. "This outlines some of the corporate services we offer."

He had to hand it to her. She didn't miss a trick. "Thanks. I hope to see you soon."

"I hope so, too, Peter." And impulsively, she leaned forward and kissed his cheek. "You look way better than you deserve to look."

He grinned back at her. "So do you."

"LOOK, IF WE'RE celebrating crystal, I want everything crystal," Kit insisted. "I want this ballroom to look like the palace at Versailles. Mirrors on every wall, Waterford chandeliers—" she calculated rapidly "—let's say thirty."

"But the weight. I'm not sure…"

"Figure it out. See what we need to do to support them."

She was typing notes into her PalmPilot. Cristal Champagne? Too obvious? Too expensive for the client's budget? Still, when you unveiled a new romance collection of stemware, including an erotic collection designed for lovers and newlyweds, where else would you host the product launch but at Hush?

She fingered a heavy crystal goblet with twining naked figures around the stem and thought suddenly of her and Peter sipping champagne in the jetted tub. She missed him with an ache that pierced her.

Ridiculous. It was a weekend of sex with a man who

needed to know he could be a casual sex buddy in a city where such relationships were commonplace, but he could never be a serious part of her life.

He loved her, he'd said. She'd fallen for that line once before and look where she'd ended up.

She turned and went back to her notes. Champagne in a crystal fountain. Was there such a thing? There must be, and if it existed, she'd find it; everything in this room was going to be crystal if she could rent, buy, borrow or invent it, from the serving trays to the lights, to huge vases they'd fill with flowers. She'd asked the florist to try and combine some of the crystal pieces into the arrangements themselves. He'd grumbled, as usual, but she knew he'd come through for her. She was concocting a laser light show that would be an artistic representation of the prism effects of crystal. It was expensive, and a little dicey in this ballroom, but it would have a great wow factor.

Her cell phone rang.

She smiled and answered, "Kit Prestcott."

"I miss you."

The arrogance of the man. No "Hi, it's Peter Garson," just "I miss you," as though she'd know exactly who it was from the sound of his voice. Which, of course, she did. She wasn't childish enough to play games and pretend not to know who was on the phone, even though she was tempted.

"What can I do for you, Peter?"

"Have dinner with me."

"Sorry, I can't. I'm busy."

"I haven't said what night yet."

"Oh," she held the phone with her chin against her shoulder so she could gesture to the hotel maintenance guys trying to figure out how to hang thirty chandeliers. "I want them in three rows," she yelled up at the ceiling, her arms gesturing to illustrate approximately where.

"Too heavy," Mario, the foreman, yelled down at her. "They'll fall and break." He was so negative. Honestly.

"Experiment with something that doesn't break."

She reshuffled the phone and went back to Peter. "Sorry, I'm up to my neck here."

"Would lunch be better?"

She stood there, wanting to say yes, in the same way she wanted to believe in him again, but knowing she couldn't. "I'm pretty busy this month. Why don't I call you when I have some time?"

There was a pause. Then he said, "The thing is, it's business."

"Business?"

"Yes. I want to plan an event at Hush."

Suspicion had her frowning into her phone—something she never did. "What sort of event?"

"That's what I want to talk to you about. I want a—spectacle, a party, a—I don't know, a shindig—that will introduce our services to prospective clients in a memorable way."

She kept her eye on the workers grumbling and shaking their heads. What? Did they think because she was talking on the phone she was blind to how negative they were being? And she could imagine the names she was being called over there. "Why Hush?"

"Shouldn't you be telling me why I should choose Hush?" Warm humor laced his words, and she wanted to lean into the sound of his voice.

"I'm…we're pretty busy."

"My dates are flexible. Why don't I come down and meet with you over lunch."

Two guys had managed to climb on ladders overhead and were poking around up in the ceiling area and looking pessimistic.

"All right." Piper would kill her if she turned away business. She pulled up her calendar. "When were you thinking of lunch?"

"Today."

"Today? But—"

"I checked with some woman who answered your phone and she didn't see any bookings for today."

"That's because I'm working through lunch."

"How about a quick one? I'm in the neighborhood." Her cell phone sounded funny, as if his voice was echoing. She glanced up and Peter was standing inside the door, his phone stuck to his ear, staring at her.

Her foolish heart leapt in her chest. She snapped her cell phone closed. "So I see."

He stepped closer, looking crisp and sexy in a suit that had to have been tailored in Europe, a shirt whiter than snow on the Alps and a tie with geometric shapes on it. His shoes were Italian leather, and somebody had spent time recently at the shoeshine.

A thin leather briefcase hung from his fingers. She was shocked at how badly she wanted to take him.

Now that she'd regained her equilibrium, she realized how much she'd enjoyed her weekend with Peter. Everything but the rehashing of old history.

"Well?" he said, a half smile playing over his lips as though he'd been reading her thoughts.

She glanced at her watch, stalling for time, then made up her mind. "I don't have a lunch date today. I'd planned to work through the day on the setup for this crystal event. But, business is business. If you're okay eating in the hotel, then I can sneak away for a bite."

"Perfect."

She nodded. Then yelled up to Mario the grump, "I'll be around the hotel. I'm on my cell."

She got the usual grunt in reply.

"I gave you the tour of the ballroom when you stayed here last weekend," she reminded him. "This is where we hold most of our corporate events."

"It should do nicely. How many does it hold?"

"At full capacity, we can accommodate two hundred and fifty. Of course, we can also add temporary dividing walls to break it down into two smaller ballrooms."

He stood close to her and she got the faintest hint of his aftershave.

"It looks like an ice palace," Peter said, watching as the guys wrestled huge mirrors.

"I'm going for the Versailles look. We'll see."

"Always going for the wow factor, huh?"

An uncomfortable prickle itched its way down her spine and Piper's words came back to haunt her. There was the wow factor and then there was the kapow of disaster. She glanced up at the men shaking their heads above her and muttering and said, "Just a second."

She crossed to where Mario was muttering in Italian. It sounded like he was counting his rosary. "Mario, maybe you're right. How many chandeliers are you comfortable with?"

He stared at her, his eyes narrowing slightly. Then he glanced up again. "Five," he said.

"Five?" She wouldn't have Versailles, she'd have Ivana Trump's living room.

"Five…maybe ten," Mario conceded.

"Okay. I can live with that." Then she shot Mario her most conciliating grin. "Especially if it was ten."

"Do my best," he said.

Okay, so maybe the effect would be a little dimmed, but did she really want crystal crashing down like a glacial avalanche?

No. She did not.

"Well?" she said to Peter. "Shall we?"

He followed her out of the ballroom. "Amuse Bouche?" he asked.

"Let's start in my office. We can talk about your ideas." If he actually had any.

"Sure. That sounds great."

"How's work going?" she asked, as they took the elevator down to her office. That suit was giving her fantasies the way erotic lingerie got to men.

"It's good. But I need to introduce our services and some new innovations." He glanced at her and grinned. "I'm looking for wow."

"You came to the right place."

16

KEEP IT COOL, keep it business-like, Peter reminded himself as Kit led him into her office. Public Relations, it said on the door. The door was etched glass, not as fancy as the doors in the main hotel areas, but with art deco styling. Even in the basement, Piper wouldn't go with cheap, boring decor.

She ushered him in ahead of her and shut the door. "Why don't you tell me what you have in mind?" she said, gesturing to his briefcase. She didn't sit behind her desk, but sort of leaned against it, silently inviting him to stand beside her and show whatever he'd brought along.

He stood beside her and felt the warmth coming off her body. She wasn't one for heavy perfume, but her skin smelled of one of those stores that sell botanical products. She smelled of lemon and something spicy.

She shifted slightly beside him and her bare arm brushed his suit jacket. She wore a pale blue sleeveless top, a paisley cotton skirt and funky little sandals. There was a turquoise pendant on a chain around her neck, and matching earrings hung in big triangles from her ears.

Even though summer was ending, she had the light freckles that said she'd spent some time in the sun over the last weeks.

He opened the case, withdrew a sheaf of papers and laid

them on the desk. "I thought I'd share our target market strategies with you and see if you've got any suggestions."

"All right. I'll read it this afternoon and start thinking of ideas."

"Great. Thanks."

"Why don't you sit down?" she indicated, not one of her visitor chairs, but the one behind her desk. Heat was coming off her and he caught a scent that was deeper than the fruits and spice of her beauty product. It was a scent he knew and loved. Hers. When she was aroused.

He glanced at her in surprise, but she merely gestured to the chair. He walked around the desk and sat.

"I've been thinking about us," she said, walking around and hoisting a hip onto her desk.

"You have?" After the way they'd left things so unresolved on the weekend, he was delighted she was bringing up the very subject he'd sworn to avoid.

"Yes." Her voice was husky, low. "I was thinking we could help each other out." Before his bemused gaze, she slipped her hands under her skirt and eased her pale purple panties down her long, sun-kissed legs. She stepped out of the panties and neatly tucked them into her desk drawer.

His mouth went dry as his entire body sprang to attention. "Help each other out," he managed.

"That's right." She leaned over him, her lips hovering inches from his mouth. He saw the black flecks in the depths of her eyes, the dusting of freckles on her nose, pale lip color that he wanted to kiss off her mouth. She reached for his belt buckle.

The door of her office was closed, but it was glass. Anybody could see inside. They were partly shielded by

Kit's desk, and he doubted this was a high traffic area, but still. Kit surprised him.

She undid his belt while blood pounded to his groin, making him light-headed with the sudden transfer from his brain. She flipped his shirttails out of his pants, undid the button and then eased the zipper of his fly over his sudden, and very eager, erection.

Her hand was around him, warm and firm, squeezing him gently but with purpose. "Kit, I…" She stroked him and he lost all power of speech. In some part of his brain, he registered that there was something wrong with this scenario, but it was the tiny, evolved part, and it was soon silenced by the overwhelming Yes! of being surprised by sex.

He reached up under her skirt, wanting to touch her, see her, but she wasn't in the mood for toying and she let him know it by releasing his cock and yanking at his pants until they were down to his knees. He was fully dressed up top, to the knot in his tie. He made a motion to take off his suit jacket, but she stopped him. "I love that look on you," she said, letting her lust-darkened gaze travel from his business top to the erection emerging from between the two sides of his shirt.

Once more she grasped him and this time when he slipped his hands under her skirt it was to grasp her hips and nudge her onto his lap.

From the same desk drawer where she'd tucked away her panties, she drew out a condom. That was typical of Hush. It was certainly a safe-sex hotel, even down here in the business section. She had him sheathed in a second and then she sank onto him, tight and wet. And hot. Oh, so hot.

"We always fit together so perfectly," he said, feeling a rush of tenderness as he cupped her hips and held her against him. She moved, and he moved. The office chair had pretty good suspension, for it supported them, rocking with their increasingly frenzied coupling.

He let Kit find her rhythm and he held on as she rode him, rocking her pelvis so that she was stimulated both inside and out.

He wanted to bare her breasts, but knew he wouldn't. He didn't even let himself touch them, loving the idea that they were so prim and proper from the waist up, and so down and dirty below the desktop.

He watched her lovely face become passion-pink, her eyes darken and her breathing grow ragged. Not wanting to mess up her clothes, he found, as she had, that he liked seeing her in her work getup even as they screwed each other silly. He only touched her below the waist. Her legs, her hips, and finally, he slipped a hand between them to where their grinding bodies met. Her curls were damp, her clit slick with her own juices. He wanted to throw her on the floor and bare her body, he wanted to lick every inch of her, push his tongue up inside her the way she liked it. The fact that he couldn't do any of those things only made him thrust up inside her, deeper and higher.

They were both panting.

Her head went back and crazy sounds emerged from her mouth. He rubbed a little faster, feeling her begin to quiver. He could tell from her increasingly frenzied movements and the inarticulate sounds she was making that she was close. Good, because so was he.

She clutched at him with one hand, knocked her keyboard with the other so all the Happy Faces on her screen saver ran for their lives. The document revealed showed twined naked bodies—see-through bodies.

"You were viewing porn?" he panted.

"Erotic stemware," she gasped. "Client."

Her internal muscles were beginning to milk him and his love for her, his gratitude that she'd let him back in her body and her life, and his intense level of horniness were taking their combined toll. "I can't hold on much longer."

"Stay with me." She clutched him, kissed him wet and deep, her tongue driving him as wild as her gyrating body.

He held on, gritting his teeth, rubbing her magic spot, until he felt the tremors begin to rock her harder. Her body clenched against him and she used his mouth to stifle her cries as her body spasmed against him and around him. With a low, heartfelt moan, he let go, riding that glorious rush along with the woman he loved.

"Oh," she said, staring down at him with a self-satisfied expression. "That was…"

"Amazing," he said and kissed her. He took the time to do it right, kissing her long and slow until she pulled away with a slight giggle. "We'd better clean up before somebody catches us," she said, going back into that amazing desk drawer of wonders for tissues and wet wipes.

He tried to hold her hand as they left the office but she batted him away. "Stop it. I'm at work."

A little of his heady pleasure faded. In the restaurant, the lunch crowd had thinned, making it even more private. He ordered some fancy Amuse Bouche version of a steak sandwich, feeling the need for protein and red meat. Kit had the daily fish and a salad.

While they sipped Perrier, waiting for their food to arrive, he reached forward and touched the edge of her fingertips with his, liking even this tiny connection of his skin with hers. His body still buzzed from the sex, but it was intimacy he wanted right now. The kind that exists between soul mates, that had always existed between them.

"How would you like to go to Cape Cod this weekend?" he asked her.

"Sorry, I've got plans."

"What kind of plans?" he asked, stung. "We both work all week. I figured we'd see each other this weekend."

She stared at him as if he were dumber than the fork she was currently toying with. "In what universe do you think my weekend plans are any of your business?"

"In the universe where our lunch date begins with sex in your office chair."

She leaned closer, so close he could see the line where he'd kissed her lipstick mostly off her mouth. "Have you ever heard of the term bed buddy?"

If she'd shot him with a twenty-two, he couldn't have been more shocked. "Of course I have. And that is not what we are. I love you. I want back in your life."

"Then you are doomed for disappointment. I loved you once, Peter. I won't be that stupid again. I enjoy your company, the sex is great. I've been thinking that we could help each other out. I realized last weekend how much I miss having a decent lover in my life." She sent him a sizzling glance. "And you are certainly that. If you want an uncomplicated relationship until one of us hooks up in a significant way, then give me a call."

"You don't mean that."

The look she sent him was cool and controlled. "I'm not the woman you knew in college. I'm older and a lot smarter. I'm in control of my own life and my own pleasure. Yes. I mean every word."

Since lunch arrived at that moment, he didn't have to reply, which was just as well since he couldn't think of anything, anyway. He knew in his gut that she was lying. No one changed that much in three short years. But how did he get through to her? How did he let her know he was now more than ready, anxious in fact, for the very commitment that had sent him running?

How did he make her trust him again?

He ate because he was hungry, but with none of the pleasure he'd felt twenty minutes ago. Kit didn't seem to have the greatest appetite, either, picking at her food, so he thought she was a lot more perturbed than she was letting on. She usually enjoyed food with the same up-front honesty she enjoyed sex.

"Have you ever had one before?" he asked her.

She glanced up, a reddish leaf of lettuce hanging from her fork. "Had what?"

"A bed buddy."

"That is really none of your business," she said, dropping her gaze to her lettuce and shoving it in her mouth.

Which answered the question as well as if she'd simply said no.

A small measure of relief spilled through him. She hadn't changed so very much, and she was yanking his chain for reasons of her own, reasons he didn't think were that difficult to figure out.

"Fine," he said, deciding to call her bluff.

"Pardon?"

"Fine. I agree. Sex buddies it is." If the woman believed she could have a casual relationship with a man who'd already told her he loved her, with the man she was in love with, even if she was in big-time denial, then he was willing to play along. At least until she came to her senses.

She swallowed, then sipped water. "All right then. Good."

"So, how does this work? We call each other when we want sex?"

"Pretty much. And if the other is busy or doesn't feel like it, then it's no big deal."

"Agreed," he said formally, wondering how long she thought she could keep this up. He hoped it wasn't long, because he certainly couldn't keep up any pretense that his feelings were casual. Not with Kit.

"So," she said, after the silence grew heavy, "what kind of event are you planning at Hush?"

He blinked, wondering what she was talking about, then slowly it came back to him. The flimsy excuse of an event that he'd pathetically, if gratefully, accepted from Piper. That he should hold a PR event at Hush.

"Basically, I want to invite our firm's top clients and some prospective clients to an evening they'll never forget. In a good way."

"Is it also a way of introducing you to these big shots?"

"Sort of. But I don't want to be the star attraction or anything."

She toyed with her food for a bit. "I'm not sure this is the greatest idea, you know. Hush has a certain…reputation."

"Hey, don't try to blow me off. Remember, I helped you out of a jam. I'm counting on you to help me out, too."

Her head jerked up and she stared at him. "When did you help me out?"

Now it was his turn to look shocked. "I got you an escort for Funny Girl, didn't I?"

"You tried to set my fantasy weekend winner up with a gay man."

"Giles isn't gay," he reminded her.

"You thought he was when you set them up," she said.

"I still think you could be a little more grateful."

She tried to look irritated for another moment and then suddenly he saw her mouth quirk into a smile and a dimple appear in her cheek. "Actually, I am grateful. That fantasy weekend promotion was a roaring success. We practically had to throw those two out of their suite on Monday. As far as I know, they've moved the affair to his penthouse. Irene's so happy she sent me flowers."

"And Giles?"

Her smile widened and then she broke into laughter. "He sent me flowers, too. I swear those two are crazy in love."

He was mildly pleased that his inadvertent bit of matchmaking had paid off so well. Even more pleased that the hotel's fantasy weekends really seemed to work. "Crazy in love like we are?"

Her sunny humor disappeared as though a storm cloud had rolled in front of the sun. "Like we used to be."

"Fate's giving us another chance, you know."

"I believe that we make our own fate, just like we make our own luck. We may be sleeping together, Peter, but nothing's changed."

"Oh, everything's changed."

She glared at him, then pushed away her half-empty plate. "Dessert?" she said brightly.

"I had mine, before lunch," he reminded her, rubbing his knee against hers under the table. She might pretend to herself and to him that she could sleep with a man she didn't care about, but he preferred to believe otherwise.

She smiled, but didn't reply. Maybe he'd shocked her

by so easily agreeing to her dumb-ass plan. Fine. He'd win her back using every weapon in his arsenal, and he figured the most potent of those was his intimate knowledge of her character.

"I need to get back to work," he said, reaching for his wallet.

"Right," she said. "Lunch is on me," she told him.

"But my fantasy weekend is over."

"And now you're a public relations client." She had her professional PR lady face back on. "Don't worry. I'm going to design you a fantastic event, but the hotel will make money off it, too."

"It's a win all around, then," he said lightly, wondering what she'd do if she knew that Piper had suggested this little stunt to help Peter spend more time with the woman he loved.

Bash both their heads together probably.

"Thank you for lunch, then," he said, as she rose.

"You're welcome."

There was a second's awkwardness. He'd been inside her body less than an hour ago, muffling her cries of ecstasy with his mouth. He held out his hand formally.

Giving him a raised eyebrow, she shook his hand.

"I'll look forward to hearing from you," he said and turned away. Thousands of people said, or typed, or text messaged those words every day in a business context. But he liked the fact that when he said them, he was talking about being at Kit's sexual beck and call, and she knew it.

Things weren't going smoothly in his campaign to win back the woman he'd so foolishly lost, but he had a strong feeling they were going to get interesting.

KIT CALLED PETER on his cell phone at the end of the day on Friday. Her crystal event was in full swing, and it was a smashing success in every way except any actual smashing.

After her lunch with Peter, she'd gone back to the ballroom and toned the room down even more and now she was delighted with the effect. It wasn't Versailles so much as a crystal wonderland in miniature. She loved it, and even better, no one was muttering dire warnings of disaster. She'd even found time to read Peter's report and formulate some ideas.

"Peter Garson," he said, and as easily as always, his voice made her pulse quicken.

"Peter, it's Kit."

"I hope you're calling because you feel like sex," he said, lowering his voice to an intimate murmur. "You know, I think I love this idea of yours."

She hadn't felt like sex. She'd been thinking of going home, brewing tea, having a long, hot shower, a simple dinner and crashing. But his words brought her body to immediate, insistent life.

"That's not why I'm calling," she said, determined to keep the upper hand in this affair or whatever it was.

"Too bad."

"I've been thinking about your event. I have some ideas."

"Great. Do you want to talk about them over dinner?"

Did she? Of course she did, because dinner would lead to his place or her place, which would lead to making love through the night and sleeping late in the morning, sharing the paper over coffee, cooking breakfast together…all the little intimacies she knew so well. All of which could lead so easily to her and Peter spending another entire weekend together. Casual relationships only worked if you kept them casual, she reminded herself.

She was playing with fire, as she knew perfectly well. Right now she was in control, but she had to be very careful or she could end up burned a second time.

Letting a man break your heart once was a tragedy. Letting the same man break your heart twice was stupidity.

"I can't tonight," she said. "I've got an event here at the hotel. I thought maybe I could e-mail you some suggestions and we could talk them over on Monday."

"Not sure what time I'll be back Monday. I'm at Cape Cod this weekend, remember?"

Her chest felt a little hollow. He'd invited her to go with him and she'd said no. She wondered who was going in her place.

Not that it mattered, of course. Casual. That's all they were to each other. No questions, no answers. She was the one who'd set the rules, so she could hardly feel shocked that he was going ahead on a fun weekend without her, now could she?

And dinner tonight probably meant nothing more than dinner. Or dinner and a quickie. While she'd been trying to avoid being pulled into spending the weekend with him in New York, he'd been mentally packing for Cape Cod. Without her. Not the greatest boost to a woman's ego.

"Um, fine, sure. I'll e-mail you the notes, anyway. Give me a call when you get some time next week."

"Thanks."

"Well," she said, "have a good weekend."

"You, too." He sounded as if there was a smile in his voice.

17

KIT SPENT THE WEEKEND feeling irritable. The air seemed muggy, dusty and hot. Too hot for September. She bet Cape Cod was cool and breezy, still nice enough to sit outdoors in shorts during the day and cool enough for a fire at night.

She imagined Peter and some nameless, faceless woman cavorting in some adorable shingled saltbox and threw herself into an exhausting weekend of partying. In a way, it was work. She stayed abreast of all the clubs, the restaurants, the social scene. She knew who was marrying whom, expecting a baby, planning the next big charity ball. Hush was starting to get some nice parties, and some of the avante garde business events were showing up in their ballroom.

Also, these people were her friends, and she needed to remind herself that she loved being young, single and trendy. She wasn't any designer's muse, nor was she rich enough to buy every designer item she wanted or put her name on waiting lists for the newest, hottest Gucci bag.

However, she had a certain flair, and since she was seen everywhere and photographed all the time, she got a lot of presents. "Valentino thought this would look great on you for the record producer's party at Hush on Friday," and poof, a bag with a great dress dropped into her hand.

"You looked fantastic in the photo with Karl's jacket. He sends his love and one of the new shawls. Nobody can get them. Kiss-kiss."

So she went, she wore, she whirled through another crazy weekend. She was more happy than usual to have her picture taken—especially with the French heir to a vineyard on Saturday night and then even later Saturday night at Seven, the nightclub of the nanosecond, with a hottie from L.A. who'd started hitting it big with his recording career.

Naturally, she intended to celebrate the vineyard heir's Beaujolais nouveau at Hush next season. And any guy who was about to launch a record career simply had to be seen at Hush.

Sunday, she woke late and a little bleary-eyed. She organized her dry cleaning, watered her plants, cooked herself a decent breakfast and phoned her mother. Then she was off to May Ellison's bridal shower.

May was as pretty and fresh as those flowers she loved so much. Who'd have thought that a guy who penned such terrifying tales as Beck Desmond did would fall for someone so soft and sweet?

She shook her head. There was no accounting for love. Since she was a practical woman, and had some experience, she made sure her gift was the kind of thing May could still use even if the wedding didn't come off. She bought her a pretty silk peignoir set in floral silk. It was the sort of soft, dreamy thing May would love.

All the time, a sort of restlessness, like the ocean off the coast of Cape Cod, pounded away at her.

Monday, she had the satisfaction of seeing not only her picture, but also her name a few times in the gossip columns. Probably, Peter would never read them, but she was glad they were there anyway. Whatever he'd been up to in Cape Cod, all he had to do was scan the *New York Post* or the *Daily News* to see that she'd been busy too.

Tuesday morning, she was just bowing the Japanese Tourist Board members off the Hush premises after giving them an exhaustive tour, when Giles Pendleton strolled in looking as impeccable as ever.

"Giles," she said, walking forward to kiss his cheek. "What a nice surprise."

"I'm delighted to see you, Kit. I wanted a word."

"Of course." She led him to a quiet corner and they sat. "Would you like some coffee or something?"

"No thanks. I need a favor."

"I'll do what I can."

He reddened slightly and said, "It's a little personal."

Oh, he was so sweet when he was embarrassed. She lowered her voice even though there was no one for miles who could hear them. "We can be very discreet here at Hush."

"The thing is, well, I want to book the Oscar suite again. For Irene and me."

"Okay." This didn't seem so outlandish a request.

"I've got to go back to London for a few weeks. Irene…" He looked off into the distance for a moment, and she thought of the dashing prince sweeping the wisecracking Cinderella off her red Keds. Who could ever have picked this one? "Well, I don't think she really believes that my feelings for her are true."

"Ah," she said.

"She's being very brave and funny and saying absurd things like maybe we'll 'hook up' next time I'm in town. Do I look like an electric fixture?"

She bit back a smile. "No. Not at all."

"I'm not the sort of man who 'hooks up' and frankly, for all her bluster, I don't believe Irene is, either."

Kit thought of her own attempt at convincing a man she only wanted him for casual sex. At the time, she'd thought she meant it, but she'd only had to think of him shacked up with some other woman all weekend to realize her words were a lie. She didn't want casual sex with Peter any more than Irene wanted it with Giles.

She wanted the fairy tale as badly as Irene did. And she was twice as much a fool to want it from a man who'd jilted her.

She blinked and forced herself to concentrate on Giles. "So, you're going to London and she doesn't believe you'll come back for her? Is that it?"

"That is precisely it."

"And what am I supposed to do to help?"

"I'm leaving tomorrow. I want the hotel to deliver sixteen perfect red roses to Irene. She's heading back to Ohio, so to her home address."

"All right. Sixteen?" she asked, wondering if she'd heard him right.

"Yes. Sixteen, because that's the number of nights I'll be away." He was looking embarrassed again, and she could see that all this romance was hard on him. And she adored him for doing it for Irene.

"With the roses, I'd like to enclose the booking slip for the suite for the night I return and three days following."

She nodded, making a note on her PalmPilot.

Giles dug into his coat pocket and pulled out a sealed envelope. "Would you have that delivered, as well? Perhaps tucked into the hotel folder?"

"Of course," she said, taking the envelope. It was

cream vellum and expensive looking. The word Irene was written in a looping scrawl in what had to be fountain pen ink. Wow.

"Giles," she said, knowing it was totally inappropriate of her to ask, but needing to know in the most urgent way, "how can you be so sure?"

"Sure of what?"

"About Irene?"

"Oh, sure that I love her, you mean?"

"Yes. If that's not too personal."

"I've never known an American who didn't ask a great number of personal questions." He shook his head. "Extraordinary, really. But I don't mind answering." He paused to lean back in the seafoam-green chair. "Except there is no answer, is there?"

"There isn't?"

"No. I suppose it really is fate or magic or something."

"Do you think there is only one person for everyone?"

He looked sad for a moment. "I thought there was only one for me, but as you know she died. And, it took me a while, but I accepted that she was gone and I'd always be alone. Now I believe I'm getting a second chance."

"Second chance," her words echoed in her throat.

"I spent twenty years in love with a woman who could not acknowledge me in public. Twenty years of secrets and silence. Irene—" he looked up and quirked a brow "—well, she's certainly not silent. When I'm with Irene there is no question that I am with a woman who is happy to be seen and heard and who wants to be with me. I don't have to share her."

He smiled at her, his eyes crinkling. "I was fairly certain before that I'd fallen in love with Irene, but the weekend in Cape Cod was…amazing."

"Cape Cod? You were in Cape Cod?"

"Yes. We were awfully sorry you couldn't come. Peter was going to cancel, but we insisted he come along. He didn't relish playing gooseberry, I can tell you."

"Playing gooseberry?" she asked, confused.

"Third wheel, if you like."

"You mean, he was there alone?"

"Of course he was alone. If he didn't bring you, who would he bring?"

"I can't imagine," she said faintly.

Giles looked at her for a moment, then leaned slightly forward. "I don't share the American mania for divulging all one's private business, or prying into other people's as a rule, so I'll content myself with saying that Peter told me about your past."

"He did?"

"Yes. He was a fool ever to let you get away."

"He did, though."

"I think you're still in love with him." She opened her mouth to argue, but he said, "And I know he's in love with you. Don't punish him so much for past mistakes that you end up missing out on a lifetime of happiness, will you?"

"But how can I ever trust him again?" she asked, voicing the question haunting her.

"There are no guarantees, my dear. That's what trust is, faith in someone without any proof."

He glanced at his watch. "I must run, I'm afraid. Awful lot to do today. You'll put all that on my account?"

"Yes, of course."

He rose. "Oh, and a couple of dozen red roses waiting in the room when Irene arrives."

"Certainly," she agreed, pulling her scattered

thoughts together with an effort. "I'm guessing you'll want champagne chilling?"

"Mmm. Definitely. Glad you reminded me. I'll have my driver run over a couple of bottles from my cellar." He glanced down at her. "Not that there's anything wrong with the wine list at Hush, of course, but one has one's preferences."

"Naturally," she said.

"Right then, I'll be off."

"Have a good trip." She smiled and kissed his cheek again. "And good luck."

He gripped her shoulders for a minute and looked down at her. "You, too."

18

So, PETER HADN'T HAD company in Cape Cod. Kit made the arrangements Giles had requested, unable to quell her feeling of satisfaction.

She returned to her office, closed the door and called Peter. When he identified himself, she said, "Are you alone?"

"One second."

She heard a murmur of voices and then the click of a closing door. One thing about Peter: he caught a sexual innuendo the way Barry Bonds caught a pitch. "I'm all yours," he said, his voice rich and low.

She let herself enjoy the moment, his voice in her ear, the tug of attraction between them. "How'd you like to be all mine tonight? My place? Say seven o'clock?"

"I could work that into my schedule," he said. "Can I bring anything?"

"A bottle of massage oil. I hope you still give those fantastic back massages."

"I'll do my best to melt *all* your tensions away."

She crossed her legs against a surge of lust that warmed her. "I'll see you later, then."

"Wait." His voice stopped her from ending the call.

"Yes?"

"I've got other massage clients tonight so I won't

want to waste any time. I'd like you to be ready for me when I get there."

Oh, she was all ready now. She swallowed, trying to keep the breathiness out of her voice, but it was hopeless. "What do you want me to do to be ready for you?"

"When I arrive, I'd like you to be naked."

"Naked?"

"That's right."

"I'm to come to the door naked?"

"Yes."

"What if it's the super? Or a pizza delivered to the wrong door?"

"That could be…awkward."

"Awkward? It would be mortifying. It could be my skuzzy neighbor Bernard who would like way too much to see me naked."

"I see your problem," he said. "But I really do need you to be ready." He seemed to be thinking, and the pause lengthened. She recrossed her legs knowing that she was going to be a jittery, aroused mess until seven.

"You can wear a robe," he finally decreed.

"A robe."

"But nothing on underneath."

Her skin prickled all over and she shivered, not with cold but with heat. "Anything else?"

"Yes. Light candles."

"For a massage?"

"In case the electricity goes out in your building. I won't have to waste time finding another light source."

"You're very efficient," she said, rolling her eyes.

"I appreciate your cooperation."

"I'll be ready," she said, and clicked off.

By seven o'clock, she was as ready as she'd ever

been. The robe felt scratchy against her skin, rubbing her naked flesh already so aroused it was ridiculous. She lit candles, put fresh sheets on the bed, Loreena McKennitt on the CD player.

She had wine in the fridge, but drank water, preferring to keep all her senses sharp. Maybe they'd have a glass of wine…after. But no sleepovers, she warned herself. This first time would be the most difficult, and she had to be absolutely clear with Peter that their relationship was about nothing but sex. Well, they were friends of a sort, and business acquaintances now that she was putting on an event for his company, but other than that it was all about the sex.

Which seemed like a great way for a fastidious but awfully busy woman like her to enjoy regular sex without it getting in the way of a busy schedule.

Her hair was brushed glossy, and she'd pinned it up in honor of the massage, her teeth were brushed glossy, her skin was shaved and exfoliated glossy. She was ready.

At precisely seven, Peter arrived. The concierge sent him up and she stood waiting by the door.

When he knocked, she opened the door immediately. He wasn't wearing the suit she'd expected but a gray T-shirt and sweats. In his hand was a brown paper bag.

"Hi," she said.

"Are you ready?" He was brisk, efficient, a massage therapist with a busy practice.

She nodded and he entered her apartment. He took a moment to look around. "Nice place."

"Thanks."

"I didn't bring my table. Is your bed okay?"

She had to swallow before she could reply. What

was wrong with her? A little silly role-playing and she was tongue-tied and quaking with lust for this guy.

"Yes."

"Let's go."

She doubted that most massage therapists watched their patients take off their robes, or gazed at their bodies with such naked and flattering lust. But she wasn't complaining.

"Lie down on the bed on your stomach," he instructed and she noticed his voice had deepened. He was as turned on as she was.

Without a word, she pulled back the covers, intensely conscious of him watching her every move, and then stretched out on her stomach.

"I give a better massage when I'm also naked. Do you have a problem with that?"

"Uh, no."

She turned her head to watch him as he peeled out of his sweats. He was already hard, and she took a moment to enjoy the sight of him. The muscular chest, nicely defined arms, not quite a six-pack in the abs now that he was a desk jockey. Maybe a four-pack. Long legs and a good-size cock that had brought her a lot of pleasure in its time. She felt the bed dip as he straddled her, felt the warmth as he settled himself on her butt. His legs took most of his weight, but she felt him, skin to skin, warm and excited.

And then she heard the paper bag rustle as he removed the massage oil.

In a minute, she felt the first trickle of oil between her shoulder blades. She sucked in her breath at how cold it felt.

"I'll soon warm it to your body temperature," he said, soothing her.

"Mmm." She closed her eyes and put herself into his hands.

Those wonderful, capable hands began to move, long, slow strokes spreading the oil over her back and shoulders. He wasn't trained in any way, but damn, he was good. Under his fingers and palms, the tensions of the day melted out of her shoulders and neck, where she carried her troubles.

Which he already knew.

The oil smelled of rosemary, she thought, and something else. Pine? Total guy stuff, but relaxing, too. He kneaded the muscles of her back and arms, her neck and shoulders until she felt limp and heavy, but always, always, she knew what this was leading up to and her belly grew heavy with anticipation,

"Turn over," he said softly, and she did, gazing up into his eyes. He picked up the oil and drizzled a little between her breasts and started to rub. Her breasts became slippery and warm under his touch, her belly slick and gleaming, and finally he slipped those nimble fingers between her legs.

The second he touched her there, she cried out, she'd been building up to this for so long, it seemed. He rubbed oil on her clit, which was already slippery with her own juices.

Then he crawled down between her legs and put his mouth on her. Oh, it was so hot. And she was already so close. He licked her, teasing only a little, then tongued her faster, lapping at her, pushing his tongue right up inside her body. She rose, higher, until her hips were airborne, gyrating under his mouth.

"Oh," she cried. "Wait, I want you inside me," she almost sobbed. But she couldn't hold herself back, and under his magic tongue she sobbed out her release while he held her through the tremors, kissing her intimate places, kissing her thighs and then her belly.

"I wanted to come with you inside me," she complained weakly when she could finally speak. Every part of her throbbed in tiny orgasmic echoes.

"You will," he promised. Hah, easy for him. How cocky. She almost never came twice.

And then, he was leaning over her, kissing her mouth, so she tasted her own passion and a hint of rosemary. He entered her slowly, so she felt her body stretch around his hardness. Felt the echoes increase as he started to move. She wrapped her legs around him, pulling him deeper, and he rode her, then flipped them so she was riding him. Oh, and when she angled her pelvis just so, he hit her G-spot every time. And when Peter slipped a finger to touch her clit, she knew that he'd been right.

She let the delicious sensation build slowly inside her, controlling the speed and angle, staring down into that strong, sexy face. She watched as his forehead grew damp and his eyes lost their focus, until his breathing grew as ragged as her own.

She gripped his shoulders, then leaned down to kiss his mouth. And when she cried out her release, he swallowed it as she swallowed his.

She slumped, damp and slick with oil, against his chest, still making small thrusting movements because she never wanted the sex to end.

Peter stroked her hair, and then kissed her passion-swollen lips.

"You give a great massage," she informed him.

"It's easy with you. You're a naturally relaxed person."

"Thanks."

She thought about offering him a glass of wine, but then realized that she'd only start down a dangerous and slippery path if she did that. Instead, she said brightly, "So, what are you planning to do for the rest of the evening?"

There was only the tiniest of pauses before he said, "I told you, I've got a full schedule of massage patients."

She punched his shoulder. "Really."

"I'm on my way to the gym." He turned and gave her a slight grin. "For another workout."

Not wanting to be churlish and throw him out right away, she said, "Do you want to shower before you leave?"

"Nah. I'll shower at the club."

He blinked, then rolled away, disappearing into the bathroom. When he returned, he picked up his clothes off the floor and put them on with close to the same speed he'd stripped them off earlier.

"When will I see you again?" Peter asked.

"I'll call you," Kit said.

"Okay." He sounded fine.

And so Kit started her first relationship based on casual sex.

Peter certainly didn't seem to mind. In fact, when one sex session ended, he never pressed for a firm date for their next encounter.

Sure, he called her as often as she called him and she'd spend a Saturday afternoon or a passionate evening at his place, but she never slept over. Never let him sleep at her apartment.

Her plan was working great. Better than she'd thought possible. He'd taken a little bit of training, but now he didn't even try to take their relationship any deeper.

Sometimes it felt as though he were looking at her with an intensity that was far from casual, but he'd never again done anything as stupid as telling her he loved her.

She still went out on the town and was seen with the who's who of the Manhattan under-thirty crowd.

Sometimes, she even bumped into Peter. Which is how she ended up dancing with him at Incendiary. The club wasn't even new. It had been around for a while, but suddenly it had been discovered in that mysterious way of popular night spots. The evening she bumped into Peter, she was escorting Seamus O'Rourke, the *enfant terrible* lad-lit writer from Ireland. Seamus looked just enough like Colin Farrell to get him into as much trouble as he wanted—and he seemed to like a lot of trouble, as did his young bad-boy agent. They were staying at Hush, of course, and when they asked her to go to Incendiary with them, she agreed.

There was a wicked lineup outside the club when the limo drew up, which was normal. She and her guests walked to the front and were ushered in with a friendly greeting, which always made her feel a tiny bit guilty for all the poor souls still standing in line. But, she reminded herself, it was her job to get Hush guests past lineups. And if people like her and Hush VIPs didn't patronize Incendiary, it would cease to be hot and therefore cease to have lines.

She was wearing a new Carolina Herrera dress in rainbow colors that Piper had bought and then decided made her look too pale. She'd bestowed the expensive designer outfit on Kit. It wasn't the first time she'd passed down clothes she'd never worn, and Kit had learned to accept that Piper was never going to have the same respect for money that she did. So, she took the dress, which Piper decreed looked much better on her, and strapped on bright red stilettos that matched the red in the dress. She'd had her highlights retouched earlier in the week and she'd bought a new lip gloss that shimmered. Inside, the club was packed with the young and the trendy.

She knew a lot of people and took the trouble to introduce the Irish duo around. Then the three of them slid into one of the dark red leather booths. Seamus insisted she try his favorite drink, so she found herself sipping thirty-year-old Irish whiskey. Not her favorite, but she didn't want to hurt Irish-American relations, so she nursed her heavily iced drink.

Seamus tried to explain that his novels were an exploration of his particular brand of religion, which seemed to be Catholic agnosticism, as far as she could tell from his slurred tangle of speech. As she tried to listen intelligently, she became aware of eyes on her.

She glanced up to see Peter gazing at her from across the room. For a second, the noisy club fell eerily silent and she felt her heart bang, once, hard against her ribs before the moment ended and the world righted itself again.

The last time she'd seen him, he'd been naked, and kissing her goodbye at the door of his apartment. She'd wanted to stay, but hadn't let herself suggest it. And Peter hadn't asked.

After sending him a small wave, and noticing that he was in a group of more females than males, she turned her attention back to the writer.

His agent, who'd drained two whiskeys in no time, mumbled something about "seein' about the service," and ambled off. She returned to listening to the writer, wishing she could contribute something to the discussion, except that she'd only made it through half of one of his novels and found the only thing memorable was his creative use of profanities.

"Oh, my God, it is you," an excited female voice shrilled from Kit's left. One of the women she'd seen Peter with, an intellectual-looking but glamorous anorexic all in black, with square black-framed glasses, was staring wide-eyed at Seamus. "I loved *Seven Deadly Sinners.* You are incredibly talented. I can't believe you're here in New York."

Before Kit knew how it had happened, the thin woman had slid in beside Seamus, who was explaining to her, a lot more successfully than he had to Kit, what exactly his belief system was and how it influenced his work.

She didn't know quite how it had happened, but the booth was suddenly crowded with Peter's party and her own and she was sitting beside Peter, deeply aware that her casual lover's thigh was pressed warmly against her own.

When the agent returned, the booth was simply too crowded for all of them. That's when Peter asked her to dance.

Since the Irishmen were now deep in convivial talk and laughter with four attractive, interesting women, Kit slid out of the booth and let Peter lead her to a small, crowded floor and pull her against him.

"Aren't you going to thank me?" Peter said into her ear.

"For what?"

"Rescuing you from that Irish bore."

"How did you know he was boring me?"

"You do this thing when you're bored. You start playing with your watch strap. Unbuckling it and rebuckling it."

"I do?" No wonder she went through the things so fast. "Maybe it's a nervous gesture."

"Nope. When you're nervous you play with your hair."

"You seem to know an awful lot about me," she snapped.

"I've known you a long time. Like right now, your eyes are getting dreamy-looking. Know what that means?"

"I'm tired?"

"You're aroused," he said softly.

He moved against her and it was perfectly obvious he was also aroused. Whatever had been wrong between them, it had never been sex.

"Had that woman really heard of Seamus?" Kit asked him with some suspicion, feeling that a change of subject was probably a good idea.

"Of course she had. I've heard her talk about him. She loves his stuff. Maybe she wouldn't have recognized him if I hadn't pointed him out, but…"

She chuckled. "Was there an ulterior motive, or did you want to meet the famous author?"

"I wanted to dance with you."

She glanced up to find him gazing down at her with an expression she knew well.

"Just dance?"

"No."

"I've got to get up early in the morning."

"Then how about we leave now? I'll come to your place, tuck you in and set your alarm for you."

She glanced at the booth, torn between wanting very

much to go home with Peter and not wanting to abandon her charges.

"Don't worry. Lexi will make sure your author gets back to his hotel. She'll probably tuck him in bed."

It was obvious she wasn't needed, and Seamus and his agent knew how to call the limo.

"Okay."

She said her goodbyes, told the Irishmen to call for the limo when they were ready and headed out with Peter.

They didn't touch as they left the club, but the current of desire zapping between them was an almost tangible force. In the cab to her place, which they automatically chose because her apartment was closer, they stared hungrily at each other but didn't touch. She had a feeling they both knew that the second they got their hands on each other, nothing was going to stop them.

They waited until her apartment door shut behind them and then they lunged for one another.

She dragged at his jacket, yanking it off, while he unsnapped the halter strap from around her neck and shoved the bodice down with no finesse whatsoever, reaching for her naked breasts.

They were kissing, panting, murmuring crazy things. She fumbled the buttons of his shirt in her eagerness and he finally batted her hands away and did it himself.

She liked watching him undress, but not tonight. Tonight she was too eager. It felt like years since they'd made love, when it hadn't even been a week.

Her bedroom might as well have been across the Atlantic—there was no way they could make it there with need pounding in and around them. She removed the black silk tie from her waist and let the dress fall into a silk puddle, then she stepped out of her panties while he tore off his remaining clothes.

"Not the shoes," he said, when she would have unstrapped them.

So she fell back onto her living room couch, naked but for a pair of cherry-red stilettos. Peter stood over her for a moment taking in every detail.

"I really like you in high heels," he said, then he dug through his pants until he found his wallet and a condom. Good thing to be prepared, she thought, even as she wondered…but their relationship wasn't about exclusivity, she reminded herself. Except, of course, that it was for her.

He was back at her side in an instant, leaning over and kissing her, his lips hot, his body hot, the air around them snapping with heat.

Even as she craved the feel of him inside her, stoking the heat even higher, her mouth said, "So, if you hadn't bumped into me tonight, who would you have gone home with? The thin girl with the glasses?"

Peter raised his head to stare down at her for a minute. She thought she saw a spark of anger, but it was gone so fast she wasn't sure.

"Forget it," she said, mortified that she'd asked. "Sorry. It's none of my business."

"No," he said.

"No?"

"I wouldn't have gone home with the thin girl with glasses."

And then he kissed her in a way that (a) made talk impossible and (b) made thought of any kind impossible. Maybe she hadn't slept with a lot of men in her life, but she'd kissed plenty. No one, but no one, kissed the way Peter did, as though his whole universe were wrapped up in that kiss. She was as lost as she always was and when he touched her, *oh, please,* kissed her body, *oh, more,* and entered her, *oh, yes.*

She was greedy for him, all of him. She pulled and squeezed, dragging him closer, and as she arched beneath him and her head fell back in a cry, she felt him lift her even higher, so a second climax shook her even as she felt his body clench in its own explosion.

She let her eyes droop shut as her hand stroked his warm, slightly damp back. She loved the feel of his smooth, warm skin and the hardness of muscle beneath. She thought she'd never tire of him.

"Mmm," she said, feeling sleepy and sated. "Bed."

"Right," he said, pulling himself up. "You said you had to get up early. I'll get on home."

She'd meant bed with him in it. She didn't want to sleep alone all night without him wrapped around her. But she didn't say anything. He was following the rules she'd set, and that was exactly what she wanted.

19

"THAT'S THE THIRD TIME you've yawned," Piper said, reaching over to pick up Kit's watch, which had fallen to the desk when she suddenly raised her hand to cover her open mouth.

Deftly she rebuckled the watch around Kit's wrist. "I'm not used to boring people."

"You're never boring. Sorry. I didn't get much sleep last night."

Piper was instantly alert. "For the right reasons or the wrong ones?"

"We bumped into Peter at Incendiary last night," she admitted. "He came over to my place."

"Mmm, tell all. Did he do delicious things to your body until the sun rose? He looks the type who knows how a girl's put together."

Kit felt herself blushing, which was ridiculous. "He didn't stay over."

"Okay. Nothing wrong with a quickie before bed," Piper said, but her eyes were wary. "What's going on with you two, anyway? Since you were less than pleased with me for my well-meaning interference re the contest, I've been trying to stay out of it. But it's killing me. What's going on?"

"It's—" she huffed out a breath "—weird."

"Okay." Piper grinned. "My two favorite things are my sex life and the sex lives of my friends. So spill."

Kit laughed and reached across her desk to grip Piper's hand. "You're a good friend, you know. In your own interfering way."

"So?" Piper said, leaning a hip on Kit's desk and staring down at her. "Details? Or is it all too complicated?"

"No. For once, it's simple. Peter is a man I can call if I want sex. We're both single, live crazy schedules, and we're compatible in bed." Compatible didn't begin to describe it, she thought. "So, we're helping each other out."

Piper stared at her as though she'd this second grown a fig tree out of the crown of her head. "Your ex-fiancé has been demoted to a booty call?"

"I wouldn't have used that term. But yes. That's exactly what he is."

"You do understand the unwritten rules of the booty call, don't you?"

"Yes. I've been around." She glanced at Piper. "I've known you a long time."

"Ouch," Piper said, clutching her chest, then she grinned. "Oh, I did have some good ones, huh? Remember that prince?"

"Of some godforsaken country that wouldn't let him or his family on their soil? Yep, I remember him."

"He may have had no country but he was great in bed." Piper seemed as though she was wandering down her own X-rated memory lane, but suddenly she turned her attention back to Kit.

"So, you and Peter aren't exclusive?"

A pang hit. "No."

"Who else are you sleeping with?"

There was a pause. Kit twirled a curl around her finger and then, remembering Peter's words from last night, dropped the hair and folded her hands in her lap.

"I'm not sleeping with anyone else, as you know. I've barely got time for one sex buddy."

Piper gave her one of those annoying I-know-something-you-don't-know smiles that were big on enigma. "Darling, if you sleep exclusively with a man you used to be engaged to, that is not a sex buddy."

"What is it, then?" Kit wailed.

"I guess you'll have to work that out for yourself."

FOR SOMEBODY whose career was on a roll, who loved her life in the greatest city in the world and who was getting fabulous sex regularly, Kit was awfully jittery. Something felt slightly off, as though her life were a puzzle where none of the pieces quite fit. In fact, some days she felt as if the picture on the box was wrong.

Maybe she simply wasn't getting enough sleep. She'd have incredible, mind-blowing, fly-me-to-the-moon sex and then lie awake for hours in her lonely bed thinking about her lover, her career, her life, her parents, whether she'd ever have kids. Stupid things that seemed so incredibly important at three in the morning.

Peter's event was less than a week away and she was knocking herself out to make sure it was memorable. The guest list had Piper salivating because she knew as well as Kit did that those same people who were being wooed by Peter's firm were also hopefully going to be seduced by Hush.

Since neither she nor Peter were interested in the usual dog and pony show with wine and cheese and a slide show or even worse, ye olde company video, they'd gone with Manhattan's favorite excuse for a party. The charity event.

There would be no hard sell. The event was sponsored by Peter's company and she'd insisted that he be the evening's master of ceremonies. All the guests were paying a hundred bucks a head to help restore one of the oldest theatres on Broadway. Since it was also the theatre where the Tony-nominated hit, *Love Ya, Babe,* was playing, Kit had been able to arrange for the two leads in the play to present a short scene from the play at the party.

She'd decided to theme the evening around the 1920s when New York's Stanley Theater had opened its doors. She'd borrowed some movie posters and props from the hit plays of the era, and had turned the ballroom into a kind of movie set version of a Twenties theatre.

The dress code was Twenties, Jacob Hill and his staff were creating a light supper authentic to the period, and, in a flash of four-in-the-morning inspiration, Kit had hired actors to serve the food and drinks. Well, it wasn't as if most of them hadn't had experience waiting tables and tending bar.

Each actor or actress adopted a persona from the stage or screen, and she'd told them to recite actual play and movie dialogue wherever possible.

At one point, she'd planned to do a scene complete with aerial stunts. Hah, wouldn't that wow the crowd? But when she thought about the logistics, she quietly put that idea away. Sometimes, she realized, she could put on a great event without flying actors or crocodiles. This time, all she wanted was for Peter to get a good profile, some decent press and, hopefully, the accounts of some prospective clients.

The day of the event, Kit personally checked and re-checked every detail until Piper finally threw her out of the ballroom. "Go get dressed, Kit. Now."

"I'm running Cassie through her lines one more time."

"Cassie is an experienced actress, she'll be fine." Cassie and Roger were doing a scene from the first play ever produced at The Stanley. The play was so over-the-top melodramatic that Kit had coached the actors to play it up for laughs.

"Right." Kit nodded, unexpectedly nervous. "I want tonight to be perfect, that's all."

Piper smacked a kiss on her cheek. "It will be."

And it was. When Kit came back down, she wore a vintage silver flapper dress with a beaded fringe. She wore a beaded band around her head and long jet beads. She'd had her hair and makeup done in Hush's salon and the clever hairstylist had managed to curl her hair into a longish Twenties bob while the makeup artist had gone heavy on the eye makeup and light on everything else. She really did feel as if she'd stepped out of a different era.

On reentering the ballroom, she was delighted to find that Peter was already there and that he'd followed instructions. He wore a crisp tux and spats and looked so gorgeous her heart did a bit of a Charleston.

He caught her gaze on him and stopped in mid-conversation with Piper. His eyes narrowed slightly and gave her a slow once-over that made her body flame. She walked slowly toward him and he never took his eyes off her.

"You could have been a flapper, Kit," Piper said. Since Piper never believed in following rules, she'd gone for a Marlene Dietrich look. She may have been a decade out, but she looked stunning in a long, black evening gown.

"I was telling Piper how much we appreciate all

you've done. This evening is important for us. It turns out all the board members decided to come."

Kit blinked. "Aren't you an international company?"

"Oh, yeah. They flew in from Singapore, London, San Francisco, Paris and Berlin. They're having a board meeting while they're here, but they definitely flew in because of the party. I'm on the hot seat, all right."

"Nothing like a little extra pressure to add spice to an evening," Piper said. "Excuse me, I'll warn Trace to be on his best behavior."

"You look fabulous," Peter said in the tone he reserved for her.

"You look pretty fabulous, too," she said, reaching up to straighten his bow tie.

"How about a kiss for good luck?"

He didn't wait for her to agree, but covered her mouth with his. She felt the usual heat and spark flare between them. He took his time, kissing her thoroughly, then said, "I'll collect the rest of that later, in my room."

"Pretty sure of yourself, aren't you?"

He grinned down at her. "You bet."

"Kit, the chef wants to know…" and she was off in the usual rush of last-minute requests and minor panics that were an inevitable part of her job.

Within the first hour, it was clear that the event was a success. She heard a lot of animated talk and laughter, and the ballroom was so full she knew almost everyone who'd bought a ticket had actually showed up.

Excellent.

Peter was the perfect emcee. She was so proud of him. He managed to be funny without getting carried away, to mention his company without doing a sales pitch, and in general to be so charming that she wondered if she was the only woman who dreamed of going up to his hotel room after the event.

A flutter of possessive pride stirred her blood, though, because she knew she'd be in his bed later.

Considering that he was the emcee, and that this event was partly to help him launch his career here in New York, he spent a lot of time with Kit. He introduced her to all the board members of his company. When she admonished him for wasting time on her, he kissed her nose. "I'd rather impress you than the entire Fortune 500," he assured her.

She laughed and then the laugh froze as two people she knew very well, but hadn't seen in more than three years, approached.

"Mr. and Mrs. Garson?" she spluttered.

"Kit, how nice to see you again," Peter's mother said warmly, embracing her in a scented hug.

"Mom, Dad, glad you could make it," Peter said.

"Hello, Kit," Mr. Garson said, giving her a smacking kiss on the cheek. "When Peter mentioned in his e-mail that he was planning this, we decided it was time to take a trip to the Big Apple anyway. We haven't been here for years."

She was so shocked she could barely think of anything to say. "Um, what a surprise," she managed. They smiled at her with fondness. "Where are you staying?"

"Right here," Peter's dad said.

Her eyes widened. Did they have a clue what kind of a hotel this was?

Apparently they did. Peter's father put an arm around his mother's shoulders. "It's a good thing to shake things up now and then, kids," he said, looking from one to the other. "You remember that."

Did they know that she and Peter were sleeping to-gether?

"John," Peter's mother said, giving him a reproving glance.

"Well," Kit said, desperate to escape, "I'd better go check on the band." She sent them both a totally inane grin. "Nice to see you again. Excuse me."

The band was doing absolutely fine without her in-terference, so she slipped out and hid in the kitchen for a few minutes until the shock of seeing Peter's parents for the first time since her aborted wedding had sunk in.

It had felt so natural for a minute there, the four of them together celebrating Peter's success. If only... She shook her head. But that was stupid. It hadn't happened. He was a nice guy, a fantastic lover and until she met the man she still hoped was out there, he was a conve-nient lover.

The trouble was, of course, that the man she hoped was out there for her was exactly like Peter except for his ability to make and keep a commitment to a woman.

"Kit, when you go back, can you tell Roger that he has to keep his jacket on when he's serving?" One of the sous-chefs held a white dinner jacket in his hands.

With a gasp of annoyance, she snatched it up and marched back to the ballroom.

She stuffed Roger back into his jacket and did her job. By keeping a careful eye out, she managed to avoid Peter and his parents for the rest of the evening.

Until the last guest had left, and there was only her, Peter, the actors and wait staff, and the band packing up their gear. Even Piper had snuck out with Trace earlier in the evening. That party girl sure didn't party like she used to. Not in public, anyway.

Peter came up to her with a big smile on his face and caught her in a huge hug.

"Success?" she asked.

Peter glanced down at Kit and thought she was the sexiest woman he'd ever seen. Her eye makeup was heavier and somehow different than usual. He didn't know what she'd done, but he recognized it was something to do with the flapper era. The costume was sleek and sexy, and every time he'd watched that fringe sashay around her legs, he'd wanted to speed up time to the end of the evening when he could finally take her upstairs and ease that dancing dress up over her body.

Her brows rose slightly, and he realized he hadn't answered her question.

"Better than you can imagine. I've got a pocket full of cards from people who are going to give me a call next week, and all the board members seemed to be having a good time. Always important," he said.

"That's great." She glanced around. "Um, where are your parents?"

"They went to bed early." He grinned at her. "I'm pretty sure they're having a good time at Hush."

"Well, that's nice," she said. "I wish you'd warned me they were coming."

"It was sort of a last-minute thing. I guess in all the craziness, I never had a chance to mention it." He touched her arm. "They were happy to see you again."

She smiled faintly. "That's nice."

"So, anyhow, my aged parents snuck off early, Piper and Trace cut out early and it's finally our turn. I think you and I have a date upstairs," he murmured in her ear.

"I believe we do," she said.

"I've got a bottle of massage oil with your name on it."

"Oh, I definitely have some tense muscles that need work."

"Come on."

He was in one of the regular rooms tonight, but there wasn't a room in Hush that wasn't fabulous.

He watched Kit as she entered the room ahead of him. That teasing fringe had his hands itching to get under it, to Kit, hot and willing and all his.

She yawned as she got into the room and spied the big bed. "That mattress is going to be heaven. I think I've been on my feet the entire day."

Of course she had, and she'd worked herself ragged for him and his event. He was thinking of nothing but plunging into her willing body, and she was telling him she had sore feet. Time to show the lady that he was capable of putting her needs first.

He pulled the covers back and motioned for her to sit. She did. He pulled off her shoes, slowly, and then, even more fun, reached under her dress for the stockings. She hadn't disappointed him. Knowing Kit's obsession with detail, he'd assumed she'd wear old-fashioned stockings and a garter belt, keeping even her underwear authentic. She hadn't let him down.

He unsnapped the stockings and let his thumbs trail the soft, warm skin of her inner thigh as he rolled each stocking down, hearing the slide of silk against her legs and feeling the silk of her skin.

He left her wiggling her feet against the crisp sheets and flopping back on the pillows while he dragged off his jacket and tie, and then reached for the massage oil.

"Oh," she moaned, when he began to knead the soles of her feet. He dug his thumbs into the ridges of muscle, then rolled them gently into the tender skin of her instep. He pulled her toes, massaging the oil between and into each toe.

Her soft sounds of encouragement kept him going. He finished the first foot and picked up the second and worked at that. Such hard-working feet. Such a hard-working woman.

He adored her.

When he'd worked every kink out of her feet and his hands were feeling the workout, he rose and said, "I want to rub oil all…" He didn't bother finishing the sentence.

Kit was fast asleep.

A wash of tenderness spilled over him as he looked down at her. Her face was vulnerable in sleep, and so very sweet.

He knew her well. Once she was asleep, not much woke her. He looked at the dress and decided it wouldn't be comfortable to sleep in. Not only that, it couldn't be good for the dress and it looked expensive.

He went to the bathroom and washed the oil off his hands. He caught a glimpse of his own reflection and almost laughed. Talk about a big disappointment. He'd been looking forward to making love for hours.

Looked like he'd have to wait until the morning.

Back in the room, he thought, up or down? Which would get the dress off easiest and without disturbing Kit? He decided on up, and eased the dress up past her hips and waist. But no way could he get it off her without raising her shoulders. He slipped an arm behind her and lifted her torso.

She muttered something and turned her face into his shoulder. He dropped a kiss on her forehead. "I need to take your dress off, love."

"Mmm." Somehow he wrestled it off her, with her sleepy help, and then she snuggled back down. She wore a slip but no bra, so he figured that was good enough.

He took off his clothes, brushed his teeth and washed his face, then he returned to slip into bed beside her.

He leaned over to kiss her lips lightly. "I love you, Kit," he said.

"Love you, too," she murmured, so sleepy she whispered words she'd never normally say to him.

He'd wanted desperately for them to spend an entire night in the same bed and wake together, he'd wanted it so badly it had become something of an obsession, but he'd never planned that she'd sleep all night with him because she was so tired she'd passed out.

Tonight, he didn't even care.

If she was willing to mumble her love to him when her defenses were down, that had to be good. Didn't it?

She loved him. He knew it with every atom of his being. He had to be right.

He was betting his life on it.

20

"THAT REALLY WAS a fabulous event last night, Kit. You made my company look good, you make me look good and we raised a few bucks to help refurbish a theater. Thanks."

"You're welcome," she said, thinking how good he looked over morning coffee and croissants, still slightly damp from their shared shower, wrapped snugly in a Hush robe.

When she'd woken this morning, first disoriented then embarrassed, he'd refused to let her rush home to her apartment. She'd broken her one unbreakable rule and slept over. She hadn't planned to, but she had, and now she felt all the vulnerability of her position.

After shamelessly trading on his intimate knowledge of her to get her to change her mind, he'd made love to her until she didn't even remember where she lived, much less have any desire to go there.

They'd finished in the shower where he'd made her cry out with the water pounding around them and his body thrusting deeply into hers. But then, while she was in the bathroom, he'd sneakily ordered a room-service breakfast.

"I should really get going," she said.

"You haven't finished your breakfast."

"I know, but I've got a lot to do today and I'd die if

I bumped into your parents in the hotel while I was wearing last night's dress." She started to rise.

"But I want your advice."

She blinked at him and sat down again. "About what?"

"I'm doing some event planning of my own," he said, spreading ruby-colored raspberry jam on a croissant. She took a sip of coffee.

"Event planning?"

"Yes."

"Peter, you can barely handle a dinner reservation."

"I'm planning our wedding," he said in a matter-of-fact tone.

She was so stunned she simply stared at him, not even realizing her coffee cup was halfway to her mouth until she felt the hot liquid splash onto her robe. She jerked herself back to attention.

"What did you say?"

"You told me that you would never again plan our wedding, which I perfectly understand. So I'm planning it."

"Our wedding?" she asked in stunned shock.

"Yes. Will you marry me?" He gazed up and she saw such warmth there that she wanted to throw herself across the table and yell for joy. But she was older now and, she hoped, wiser.

"I can't believe you're asking me a second time."

"Actually, I don't think I asked you the first time."

She winced. "I got a little carried away."

"I know. I remember saying 'I love you,' and the next thing I was being measured for a tux."

"You weren't ready," she said, feeling a lump form in her throat.

"I'll never know if I was or not. I panicked and ran. But we'd have worked it out, Kit. We'd have been okay."

He reached forward and took her hand. "I've done some stupid things in my life. Bought Enron shares right before the company tanked, went deep-sea diving with an instructor who was drunk and nearly got us all killed, but the absolutely worst thing I ever did in my life was run out on you."

She nodded, feeling her eyes fill and not bothering to hide the fact that he'd hurt her. She was done with pretending to Peter.

"I've never stopped regretting it, not for one second. I thought I was only feeling guilty because I'd hurt you, but now I know I regretted letting you get away. I could never love another woman, because I still loved you. Always. I'll only ever love you."

"How do I know you won't run again?"

"How do I know you won't? It won't be easy, it will be life. But life is a hell of a lot more worthwhile with you in it than it ever will be without you."

She sniffed. "Where are we getting married?" He might think he could plan an event, but she already had a list going of things they'd need to do. The venue would need to be booked at least six months ahead for anything decent. Could she live with the worry for half a year? Wondering if he'd be there?

"The wedding's going to be right here at Hush hotel," he said.

"Hush?" she blinked at him.

"It seems like the perfect place to me. It's where we came together again." He winked at her. "In every sense of the term."

But she was in no mood for double entendres. Her brow creased. "You want to get married at Hush?"

"Yes. It's perfect."

"When?"

"Today."

The coffee cup would have fallen right out of her hands this time if he hadn't had the dexterity to catch it and replace it on the saucer.

"You want me to get married today?"

"I don't just want to, I've planned it."

"But, but…people don't just get married. What about the invitations? The groomsmen, the…the…"

"Boutonnieres?"

"Exactly."

"What if we just got married?"

"I could hold on to you every second until the ceremony so you couldn't run away."

"Piper's already offered to hold a gun on me until the ceremony."

"Piper knows?"

"She's your bridesmaid. Of course she knows."

He wasn't kidding. He really had done some advanced planning. Asking Piper to stand up for her. Wow. That had taken some guts on his part.

"She said she'd do it? Again?"

"Uh-huh."

"Oh, that's so sweet. She didn't even like the dress the first time."

"She likes this one. She picked it out herself."

"But what about my dress? I can't get married in—" she glanced down at herself "—a Hush robe."

"Piper's got about six dresses and every single thing in that boutique for you to choose from. The hairdresser's on call. The flowers are being done." He grinned at her. "I'm even wearing a boutonniere."

"I can't believe it. I… Why are you doing all this?"

"Because I love you. I screwed up and I need to make it right."

She sniffed again. "I can't get married without my mom and dad. They'd be so hurt."

"Of course they would. They checked in last night."

Suddenly the obvious dawned on her. "And your parents are here, too."

"Yes."

"I can't believe you are doing this."

"We're having the reception upstairs in the roof garden. May's got something fancy planned with garlands or some damn thing. The minister's performing the ceremony there, followed by dinner, cooked by Jacob Hill's own hands."

He was looking a little flustered, she realized.

"What if I say no?"

He glanced at her, and he'd never looked at her so tenderly. "Then I will be the one feeling like a prize ass with a whole wedding planned and no bride." He reached out and grasped her hand. "It would be awful, humiliating and you would have the perfect revenge. I'm giving you that. Revenge on a silver platter, or marriage to me."

"I can't believe you planned an event."

"I hope I didn't forget anything. Let's see. We're staying right here at the hotel tonight." He looked across at her and his eyes smoldered. "It feels like a great place for a honeymoon."

"Can't argue with your taste on that."

"Giles suggested we use his place in Cape Cod for our honeymoon. Later, I thought we'd go to Europe or something. But for the next few weeks, I want you to myself. I don't care where."

"I would love to go to Cape Cod."

"I know I forgot something," he said, standing and prowling the room. Suddenly he turned. "Of course, what an ass."

He put his hand in the pocket of his robe and pulled out a distinctive blue box. He opened it and then went down on one knee, looking slightly ridiculous in the robe, but not so ridiculous she didn't love him for it.

A princess-cut diamond solitaire she and Piper had admired at Tiffany's winked at her. "Will you marry me, Kit Prestcott?"

"If I don't, can you take the ring back?" He'd broken her heart three years ago, she certainly wasn't going to make a second wedding easy on the guy.

He didn't look nearly as worried as he should, in her opinion. Maybe the way she was smiling through sudden tears had something to do with it.

"No, I can't. It's already engraved. See?" She squinted to read the tiny engraving. There was today's date, their initials and the word *Always.*

"Always?"

"That's how long I'll love you."

"Oh, Peter. Me, too."

"So, will you finally marry me?"

She gazed into his eyes and let him see all the love she'd denied feeling. "What color are the roses?"

"No roses. May's doing something fancy. I left it to her, but I made her promise there'd be no roses."

"You're smarter than you look."

"I'm in agony down here waiting for you to answer me."

"I know. I'm enjoying the moment."

He slid the ring on while she was busy trying to think of more ways to keep him waiting.

"Hey, I haven't said yes yet."

"I love you, Kit."

"You already said that."

"Do you love me?"

She launched herself at him, catching him off balance so they both fell to the floor. "I love you. And if you ever so much as think of leaving me again, I will hunt you down and shoot you."

"Can I take that as a yes?"

She stretched her body over his and kissed him.

"Yes, Peter. I will marry you."

"Today?"

She laughed at the sheer delight of not having to plan the most important event of her life. "Yes. Today."

*Get ready to check into the Hush Hotel
in December 2005 with HOT SPOT
by Debbi Rawlins.
Here's a sneak preview...*

1

JACK ARRIVED AT Erotique ten minutes early, but she was already there. He knew it was Madison Tate sitting at a small table near the black circular bar. Not just because she was the only woman sitting alone. The voice on the phone matched this woman perfectly. The way she was dressed, the way she sat with her back straight and her head held high. No nonsense.

While the other women in the bar were decked out in the latest fall offerings, she dressed simply in jeans and a white T-shirt, generic, not designer. Her dark blond hair wasn't particularly stylish, either. Kind of short and unruly, and before he crossed the room, her long slender fingers pushed the stubborn locks away from her face twice.

The moment she saw him she stood and smiled. A nice friendly smile. Not the kind he usually got from women.

"You're early," she said and offered her hand.

He accepted the firm handshake. "You're earlier."

"Bad habit of mine." She reclaimed her seat, and he took the one across from her.

"My mother used to say that being prompt or early shows respect. Being late indicates you think your time is more valuable than the other person's." He didn't have the faintest idea why he'd elaborated like that. But when her mouth stretched into a beautiful smile he was glad he had.

"Your mama sounds like a wise woman."

"Yes, she was."

Madison's brows puckered slightly. "Here comes the waitress. Know what you want?"

What he wanted and what his personal trainer allowed were two different things. Ah, what the hell. "Scotch," he told the young woman in the pink vest. "Neat."

Madison waited until the waitress moved away, and then said, "You gotta admit, this place is gorgeous."

Jack glanced at the unique bar, awash in a rosy glow from the pink overhead lights. The bar chairs with the inverted triangular backs were chic and surprisingly comfortable from what he remembered of the grand opening. The entire hotel was a class act. That didn't mean he wanted to be associated with the place. "No argument there."

Her eyebrows rose. "But?"

He shrugged shoulder. "What do you want me to say?"

"That you'll do the photo shoot here."

"Why not Central Park?"

"Because it's November and you're likely to freeze you're a—behind off."

"It's not that cold yet."

"You won't say that after we've been outside for six hours." Her expression tightened, and she lifted her drink to her lips.

After a brief silence, he said, "I understand this isn't just about me. It's about the city. Isn't that the first thing people think of when you mention Manhattan?"

She gave him a funny look. "They probably think of

the Statue of Liberty." Then quickly added, "And no, we're not doing it there."

"I guess that leaves out two places."

Annoyance flashed in her light brown eyes. "I don't understand why it matters. It's not like I'm asking you to run naked through Times Square."

The waitress had reappeared. "I'm sorry I didn't recognize you earlier, Mr. Logan. Between this job and school I don't have much time to watch the news. Not that kind anyway."

He switched his gaze in time to see her before she walked away. *Not that kind.* Her words stayed behind, taunting him, reminding him of how many people didn't consider him a serious newsman. To them he was just a pretty face, delivering national news, joking with his co-anchor and providing entertainment with the television audience sipped their morning coffee.

"I have an idea," Madison said, her nervousness betrayed by the way her fingers twitched. "After our drink, why don't we go for a walk around the hotel and—"

"I've already seen it."

"All of it?"

"At the opening."

"Ah." She sighed, sinking back. "Of course." And then she straightened and leaned toward him with renewed determination on her face.

He had to smile. A moment before she spoke he could tell what she was thinking. She wouldn't make it a day in his business where everyone maintained a poker face. They had to. Never let them see you sweat. He'd learned the lesson early on.

For a second he regretted that they couldn't come to terms. Letting her take his picture might have been fun.

He shook his head. "This isn't going to work. I'm sorry I wasted your time."

"But you haven't, *Mr.* Logan…not at all."

If you enjoyed what you just read,
then we've got an offer you can't resist!

Take 2 bestselling
love stories FREE!

Plus get a FREE surprise gift!

e◆HARLEQUIN.com

The Ultimate Destination for Women's Fiction

Visit eHarlequin.com's Bookstore today
for today's most popular books at great prices.

- An extensive selection of romance books by top authors!
- Choose our convenient "bill me" option. No credit card required.
- New releases, Themed Collections and hard-to-find backlist.
- A sneak peek at upcoming books.
- Check out book excerpts, book summaries and Reader Recommendations from other members and post your own too.
- Find out what everybody's reading in Bestsellers.
- Save BIG with everyday discounts and exclusive online offers!
- Our Category Legend will help you select reading that's exactly right for you!
- Visit our Bargain Outlet often for huge savings and special offers!
- Sweepstakes offers. Enter for your chance to win special prizes, autographed books and more.

Your purchases are 100% guaranteed—so shop online at www.eHarlequin.com today!